Randy Taguchi first began writing online in 1996 and soon attracted a large following in Japan, where she is sometimes referred to as the "Queen of the Internet." She is a popular and prolific author, whose work includes a busy blog, many short stories and essays, and fourteen novels, two of which—*Outlet* and *Fujisan*—have been translated into English. She was one of the major supporters of the Fukushima Kids' Summer Camp program, which helped children impacted by the 2011 earthquake.

Her work, *Outlet* (Konsento in Japan), was commended by a leading light of contemporary Japanese literature, Ryu Murakami, as one of the best novels he had read in a decade. The novel also went on to become a finalist for the prestigious Naoki Prize.

Raj Mahtani has been a Japanese to English translator since the early nineties. He has contributed to a number of publications, including *Adweek* and *The Japan Times Weekly*, and has published several translations of novels, including Randy Taguchi's *Fujisan* and *Riku and the Kingdom of White*.

Riku and the Kingdom of White

Randy Taguchi

Riku and the Kingdom of White

Translated from the Japanese by
Raj Mahtani

Foreword by
Yuki Masami

balestierpress

Balestier Press
71-75 Shelton Street, London WC2H 9JQ
www.balestier.com

Riku and the Kingdom of White
Original title: リクと白の王国

First published in English by Balestier Press in 2016

ISBN 978 1 911221 02 9

This book was published with the support
of the Fukushima Kids Executive Committee.

Contents

Listening to Fukushima

How often do adults listen to children?

Almost always adults tell children to listen to them, not the other way around. Why? Most likely it is because they think they are more knowledgeable, having had more experiences. Yes, adults have lived longer than children and therefore it is true that they have had more experiences; however, seen through the eyes of children, the knowledge of adults is not always right; rather, it is often colored with lies, hypocrisy, and injustice.

Riku and the Kingdom of White illustrates a post-nuclear reality in Fukushima seen through the eyes of Riku, a fifth-grade boy who moves to Fukushima with his father who is to start working there as a doctor. What the boy sees is the drift of different—often selfish—thoughts and desires of the adults surrounding him. Some people, including Riku's father, say that everything is okay, while others such as Aunt Midori keep warning about health risks, without any firsthand knowledge of life in Fukushima. Tossed about and controlled by them, Riku eventually finds that adults are "surprisingly self-centered":

'It was probably better to decontaminate than to not decontaminate, but it was still kind of strange, Riku thought, that no one knew what to do with all the contaminants put out. What were the grownups thinking? Wasn't there anyone among them giving some thought to the matter of radioactive waste?

Even though adults always say to kids things like, "Think before you act," they themselves needed to heed that advice.

Riku now felt that adults were surprisingly self-centered. At one time he used to believe that, unlike children, they were bright and always looked ahead. But now, he wasn't so sure anymore.'

Taguchi Randy's decision to write with Riku as a major character suggests her wish that adults would listen to children, whose eyes are less clouded than those of grownups.

In fact, children are keen observers regarding how adults deal with environmental issues. One good example is the legendary speech by twelve-year-old Severn Suzuki at the UN Earth Summit in Rio de Janeiro in 1992. Like Riku, Suzuki questions adults' inconsistent attitudes, saying "At school, even in kindergarten, you teach us how to behave in the world. You teach us to not fight with others, to work things out, to respect others, to clean up our mess, not to hurt other creatures, to share, not be greedy. Then, why do you go out and do the things you tell us not to do?" Children's vision and voice are powerful and truthful, and perhaps for that very reason, they are often underrepresented; maybe adults are afraid of children's perceptive vision.

Since the triple disaster of earthquake, tsunami, and nuclear meltdown in March of 2011, writers and poets—established and new alike—have been exploring justice in a society which prioritizes economic growth over all other things. Some openly criticize Tokyo Electric Power Company and the government of Japan for their cover-ups of nuclear meltdown and the resultant radioactive contamination, while others question the ways of society in a subtler, personal manner. Taguchi's *Riku and the Kingdom of White* does not belong to either camp; it offers a fresh perspective from which to contemplate the future of Fukushima—and Japan—by paying attention to what and how a child sees.

Riku values compassion the most. He observes that most adults are angry, stating what they want to say and not listening. But the novel suggests a direction of hope as well, through portrayals of exceptional characters such as Mr. Nomura who is willing to listen to and play with kids, instead of preaching to or trying to control them. Mr. Nomura eventually guides Riku to "the center of his being; the place inside himself where he felt calm and cheerful."

Riku and the Kingdom of White is an invitation to listen. Only by means of learning to listen, we can cultivate the compassion needed with which to understand, and be understood by, others.

YUKI MASAMI

Professor of Human and Socio-Environmental Studies

Kanazawa University

1

MOVING TO A GHOST TOWN

I never knew geraniums were so red!

The flower plot was overflowing with them. Pressed against one another, they seemed to be leaning in to talk to each other, cheek to cheek. Though Mother had planted the seeds, they were left untended. Still, a lot had bloomed this year too.

Riku Sato stopped, wiped his face with his sleeve, smoothed out the creases of his shirt and corrected his posture. A red flower was nodding in the wind, 'Good luck.' After poking a petal and mumbling, "Thank you," he stepped over a crumbled cinder block and entered the yard.

His father was leaning against the car, in which the luggage had been loaded, vacantly gazing into the distance where the tilted house stood, apparently unaware of Riku's presence.

All the red tape, to make the school transfer happen, was finished by sometime around the end of the Golden Week holidays in May, when the new school term was already underway. Sitting there in his classroom, which was abuzz with talk of the school excursion, Riku thought: So this must be what if feels like to be a ghost.

The decision to transfer had been made at the end of last year, and Riku was resigned to the fact that he was going away. Resistance was useless, he thought. His father was being transferred to another branch. End of story.

But if only that thing never happened…

Yes, if only that thing had never happened, Riku would have started to attend his new school from April.

"This is a nightmare!" His father had said, holding his head in his hands.

The elementary school Riku was supposed to have transferred to was shut down, and the landlord of the new place they were moving to went missing. Calls to the real estate agent were attempted but the line was dead.

"Just what the hell's going on?!"

The matter of moving was no longer relevant. The entire nation of Japan was in a state of panic, and before Riku knew it, it was already May.

Perhaps, Riku hoped in his heart of hearts, his father's relocation would get cancelled too? But he couldn't speak this wish out loud. If he, in a careless moment, even got a word in edgewise, he was afraid of the backlash that would surely come flying. The grownups around him were confused all the time, after all—even more so than Riku, a mere child; his father, who rarely got angry, would raise his voice over the telephone; Riku's homeroom teacher would embrace him and spill tears like rain; and his aunt living in Yokohama was, well, frantic. The adults would even get into arguments, with their eyes raised, fox like, over differences of opinion concerning Riku.

All Riku could do—because he was still just a child—was to merely stand in the shadows of the grownups and watch things take their own course.

Please, Riku prayed, may everyone stop fighting. May they all get along again… and, if possible, may I not have to change schools anymore.

But Riku's wish didn't come true. The decision to change schools—made two months too late—was finally made.

Today was the day of parting—the day to say goodbye.

Everybody looked gloomy, as if they were attending a wake. It was because they knew where Riku was headed.

Here, in Utsunomiya too, the earthquake had wreaked havoc, destroying buildings and fences everywhere. Aftershocks also continued to occur, even to this day. They were so terrifying shivers would run down your spine whenever the ground shook. Nobody was eating the locally-grown vegetables, either, saying that the radiation level was high. As for water, everyone was buying bottled water, so the shelves at the supermarket were always out of stock. Many were also evacuating to destinations further west, believing even the entire northern Kanto region to be in danger.

Hey, did you hear? Riku Sato's moving to Fukushima.

No way! Poor guy, he's going to die from radiation exposure.

All the outpouring of sympathy only made Riku feel miserable, and so he laughed and said, with a salute, "Thank you for your good wishes. I, Riku Sato, an expeditionary party of one, do hereby vow to penetrate the world's most dangerous spot on Earth." This, for Riku, was the best bravado he could muster. All he was really saying was—*Don't worry guys, I'll be fine.*

Yuta, Riku's best friend at the time, pursed his lips and held out a wooden ball-and-cup toy, the *kendama*, grunting, "Here you go!" as if he were angry. Yuta and Riku had been thick as thieves since they began to crawl. His mother and Riku's mother were very good friends. The two boys were like true brothers, coming and going to each other's homes, eating curry rice dinners together, playing scuba divers in the bathtub, and going to Disneyland with each other's families.

The souped-up *kendama*, all lit up with its glittering, electronic illumination, was Yuta's greatest treasure. At the Christmas party three years ago, when he performed his signature *kendama* shtick—The Swallow Counter—to wild cheers, Yuta was handed, from his mother, the Kendama Grandmaster's Certificate of Merit. The Christmas tree capped with cotton snow, and the sweet smell of the pound cake baked by Riku's mother all came back to life again in Riku's mind. At that time, Riku believed he would always be together with everyone.

When Riku accepted the gift, saying, "Thank you," Yuta's nostrils flared like those of a piglet, his eyes misty with tears. Typical, Riku thought; Yuta, since way back when, had always been a crybaby.

The colored poetry card the teacher gave was lined with the words: "Do your best!" "Stay alive" and "Be well".

Riku slowly lifted his head, like a young elephant about to leave the comfort zone of his herd, and accepted the letter. His hands were full of luggage now, as all eyes fell on him.

"Thank you, everyone! So long then…"

Riku had vowed not to cry, so he tried hard to stick to his promise, but he failed, the tears began to flow; it was impossible.

At the dimly-lit entrance, while stuffing his indoor shoes into his bag, he wiped his runny nose, again and again, with the cuff of his sleeve.

"Riku!" It was Natsumi Suzuki's voice. Damn it!—Riku thought—how can I show a girl my face now, not when it's so messed up!

"What do you want…?" Riku answered bluntly on purpose. Natsumi silently held out an envelope with a picture of a giraffe.

"Read this later on, okay?" she said.

Riku bit into the envelope hovering before him and held it in his mouth.

"Riku, you twit!"

With luggage held in both hands, an envelope sandwiched between his lips, Riku watched Natsumi run away from him, her floral skirt getting sucked down the corridor like petals fluttering and scattering away. Riku shoved the letter into his pants pocket in a hurry and wore his sneakers, tapping the toes of his shoes on the floor.

Hey, wear your shoes properly! came the voice of his mother from somewhere. I'm sorry, Riku thought, but I'm in a rush.

When he zipped past the entrance and jumped out into the sunlight, even his shadow on the ground seemed sad. From the music classroom came wafting a tune being played by an ensemble of younger students, the vocalist singing the lyrics, *The Sumida River on a fine spring day…*; it was the song called "Flower." There were all sorts of other sounds, too, mingling in the air: a PE teacher barking out commands; another teacher reading aloud, her voice floating through a window thrown open somewhere. They were the sounds of his school.

Riku sensed, from the window on the third floor, all of his classmates' eyes on him. They must have been waving goodbye. But Riku was on the brink of tears, telling himself, Don't give in, Riku, man up. He then looked back, laughed, and lifted his hand, before walking slowly and normally as possible. The campus was vast, though. He walked and walked, but the school gates remained endlessly far. When he finally passed through and looked back one more time, the school seemed to be in a distant land.

"Welcome back!"

Riku's father, who had turned around to look at Riku, didn't say anything else. He just began to quietly enter some coordinates into the GPS device for the car.

The house was empty and vacant now, like a swallow's abandoned nest. Were the tatami mats so old?—Riku wondered—Was the ceiling always so high? Oh look, there's a nail hole in the pillar here, where a calendar used to hang. The place was already starting to smell like a house he had never known.

When the earthquake struck, this house had also shaken. But it withstood the disaster well, sustaining only minor damages, such as cracked walls and broken tableware displaced by the rumbling vibrations.

Riku's desk, his father's work PC and peripherals, and everyday tools and utensils were all entrusted to a moving service. At first, Riku's father was having a hard time trying to find a company willing to take charge.

He was making phone calls left and right, bowing to an invisible someone at the other end while humbly explaining his situation. Though Riku couldn't hear anything, he understood the big picture. That invisible someone was, in a businesslike manner, and in a tone overflowing with gushy sympathy, saying, "We are extremely sorry, but we no longer service that area…" or some other such thing.

After hanging up the phone, Riku's father would, without fail, lose his temper and blurt out, "Say so from the start, for goodness sake!" Then he'd shake his knee, get a little depressed, chew a stick of mint gum and mumble before pulling himself together and calling the next vendor. Whether he was treated with blunt sarcasm, or whether the fee was a little too high, he, along with Riku, had to move out. There was no arguing that.

Although Riku didn't quite understand the circumstances of his father's work, he figured that a great deal of people would get into trouble if his father didn't go.

The ten-year old Riku, though, still had a splash of pep left in him to innocently accept everything that came his way, like a puppy, so he wasn't that sad.

After checking he hadn't forgotten anything, he went out the entrance. The door wouldn't close properly, though; perhaps the earthquake had warped the fitting. He pulled the doorknob with all his might and, after a herculean effort, finally locked it shut.

"Ready?"

"Yeah…"

Farewell, my home.

Riku tossed the house keys to his father—Nice catch!

The car was stuffed with baggage. It was as if they were going camping in Fukushima—that's what it really felt like to Riku. In fact, he couldn't feel any other way, for now.

"Are you two insane?"

Aunt Midori is Riku's mother's younger sister. She was firmly against the move to Fukushima. "There's something's wrong with you, willfully going to a place where you know you'll get exposed to radiation."

It wasn't that Riku disliked Aunt Midori. She had always loved and doted on him ever since he was little, giving him lots of money every New Year's Day. But Riku wasn't thrilled at all by the idea of being taken care by her.

Aunt Midori is the sort of education-obsessed mother who'd breezily say something out of a song like, "It's better to be the one and only one, than to be number one." She loves words like talent and diligence, and believes that anyone can become a pianist if they began training at three.

Whenever Riku was in the presence of Aunt Midori, though, he would get tense and heavy-hearted.

In Aunt Midori's house, there lived two children. The older one was the eight-year old boy, Takuto, and the younger one was the six-year old girl, Akane. They were both fast talking in the way city kids usually were, and they both wore perms. Taking violin lessons ever since they were in kindergarten, the two were also now taking language lessons that focused on acquiring five languages at the same time, while also attending a private prep school for prodigies specializing in the development of right-brain thinking.

Takuto, in the presence of Aunt Midori, was an extremely well-behaved child.

He never defied her. But in secret he called Aunt Midori, "Our Board of Education." Looking grownup for his age, he was smart.

Akane was mini Aunt Midori. Her speech and gestures were exactly like her Aunt's, and, even though she was still little, she was meddlesome and a tattletale.

Aunt Midori was constantly curious about what Riku and his family were up to, as if she were competing against Riku's mother who was two years older.

"Tell me, Riku," Aunt Midori once said, "are you planning on becoming a doctor too?" Her eyes—fixed squarely on Riku's face—were gleaming, as if to be sizing him up. When she began to ask about his grades as well, Riku understood that he was being casually compared to her own children. Which is why Riku began to fear that if she were to actually take care of him, he would have to, in deference to his Aunt, act all toady and inferior to his younger cousins lest he wear out his welcome. But it was useless worrying about such a thing, since they were anyway, in reality, far superior to him.

Aunt Midori's home was a high-rise condominium in Yokohama, close to the sea. The apartment wreaked so strongly of air-fresheners that Riku's mouth would taste bitter. Her husband, a civil servant working in the tax department of Yokohama's city hall, was a black-rimmed glasses wearing man of few words. His hobby was chess and, as a member of a chess club, he had apparently been crowned champion at a tournament held in Japan. He had also taught Riku how to play the game. Whenever he cornered the king in a game of chess he would mumble, wearing a dauntless smile on his lips, "Checkmate," before proudly picking up the chess piece with his slender fingertips. Riku would be struck by how much that gesture reminded him, every time, of a super sleuth he liked on TV. The two of them—his aunt and his uncle—were very goodhearted people, but in Riku's eyes they looked like foreigners.

It was hard to believe that Aunt Midori and Riku's mother were sisters.

Riku's mother always liked to say, "The mere fact that you've been born, Riku, is reason enough for me to be happy."

It seems that Riku's mother, who was of a frail constitution, was told that she might never be blessed with a child.

"But I wanted a baby so bad," she once said. "And that's why I'm happy that you're here with me like this, that you were born."

His mother would always praise Riku and encourage him.

Surely—Riku believed—Aunt Midori had sucked up Mother's energy. Aunt Midori had never gotten sick, after all, and she stayed fit, swimming and performing aerobics once a week at the gym. Despite being super healthy, though, she kept saying, "Since that earthquake I've been so frightened I can't get to sleep at night."

She'd also say things like, "The tap water's no longer drinkable" or "I'm worried about the veggies and fish; they're all contaminated now!" What's more, she'd measure the radiation level every day with something like a clinical thermometer, remarking that it's too high or too low, and she'd call her housewife friends in the neighborhood and get caught up in discussions about buying up bottled water from the supermarket, or about ways of securing safe vegetables through mail order. She was crazy about the Internet too. Thanks to her good command of English she'd google chunk after chunk of information using English keywords, and then turn them into ammunition to torture Riku's father.

"My dear brother-in-law, you're being very selfish," she once said to Riku's father. "Don't you know that radiation exposure is extremely dangerous to a child, especially during his growth spurt? Why, the risk of getting thyroid cancer is high."

When Riku was still small, in place of his sickly mother, it was Aunt Midori who used to take care of him. And because she had been tremendously supportive in this way, Riku's father felt deeply indebted to Aunt Midori. So he never dared to snap back at her. Instead, he'd just groan—something like unnn—and fold his arms before falling silent.

Riku's father and mother met at a ski resort when they were young.

Riku's mother, who had never gone skiing before, was sweetly reassured by one of her friends who'd invited her to the trip, "Don't worry, you'll make it down somehow." Trusting those words with doe-eyed sincerity, she got on the lift, only to be whisked away to the summit, from where the mountain dropped at a sharp forty-five-degree angle. With a casual, "See ya!" her heartless friends skied down ahead of her, leaving her all alone to fend for herself. Eventually, with much reluctance, she curled herself up into a ball, looking like a snowman, and rolled down the slope, sobbing. But that was when Riku's father made his gallant appearance and said, "Excuse me Miss, can I be of any assistance?" and rescued Riku's mother, who was, by then, buried deep in the snow. Instructing her in the snowplough turn, he helped her up every time she fell—which was quite often—and safely led her down the slope to the foot of the mountain.

At that time your father was, she used to tell Riku, as cool as superman.

Riku's father was very good at skiing. He even bragged, "I went pretty far in the school championships, back in the day." Looking at the photographs of his father taken around that time, Riku realized that he was starting to resemble his father, the ski wiz, when he was young.

Riku learned how to ski from his father. He has been going on ski trips with his family since he was four, and even though his father is still a better skier than him, when it came to snowboarding, Riku believed otherwise.

His mother never got any good at skiing, though. No sooner would she ski just a little than she'd whine and flee to the lodge, where she'd wait for the two.

"I love the snow," she said, looking up at the grey skies with a smile, as Riku recalled. "The sight of pure white snow is all I need to be happy."

The skis of Riku's father and mother were strapped on the roof of the car.

"Off we go," Riku's father said, starting the engine.

"Hope there's a ski resort where we're moving to."

Father didn't reply immediately. "I'm sure there will be. We're heading to Tohoku after all, which is way up in the northeast. I don't know if you'll still be able to ski, though…"

Riku didn't hear anything further on the matter. Perhaps that stuff Aunt Midori was sputtering on and on to Riku's father about—radioactive particles—had fallen all over the ski slopes. The radioactive fallout from the explosion, Aunt Midori had said, fell together with the rain and snow. "And that's why it's extremely dangerous," she'd added.

"Look, Riku, if you like, you can live with Aunt Midori, you know."

Riku shook his head.

Wherever they were going, Riku felt he'd be better off with his father. The two of them had been holding on together for so long now. And that's why Riku thought, with genuine conviction, that he must go on helping his father from now on too.

When his father said, "Do you mind accompanying me to Fukushima? Riku was glad. He knew that his father had been consulting various people. Everyone was dead set against the idea of Riku going, but Father would patiently listen to what they all had to say. Once he thought every argument through, though, he said to Aunt Midori, "The person who understands Riku the most, and the person who genuinely lives for him is me, his father. That's why I've decided to take him along."

Aunt Midori seemed to want to say something, but Riku's father resolutely added, "Let me remind you, just for the record that, contrary to my appearances, I'm a doctor."

"No you're not! You're a psychiatrist!"

"Listen, Midori, I've graduated with a degree in medicine. It's just that the sight of blood is… well, not my thing."

If Riku's mother were there she would have sided with Riku's father. Because, at that time, he was, without a doubt, as cool as superman.

Of course, even Riku had his doubts. But he couldn't imagine living apart from his father. Riku's mother used to say, "Your father's huge as a bear, but deep down inside he's really a lonely heart," adding that he was also timid, always complaining of pain, and that the sight of blood made him faint. On top of all that, Aunt Midori would yell at Riku's father all the time. He was kind, though, and couldn't stand to ignore anyone who was in trouble. Riku respected his father for being that way—*If Dad says it's going to be all right, then it's going to be all right. Isn't that right, Mom?*

It was a clear morning in May without a speck of cloud in the sky. Father and son, having left behind Utsunomiya, their home for so long, were heading straight for Fukushima.

Two months ago, on that day—on March 11—Riku was in school sweeping the floor, just before going home, when the classroom shook violently. "Earthquake…" someone said. Everyone shot glances at the ceiling.

Minor jolts were quite common, so Riku thought it would be over soon. But the classroom continued to shake wildly. The teacher came in and shouted, "Take cover under your desks!" Riku crept under his, throwing away the broom he was holding. It was a big and long quake, with windowpanes rattling, as if a giant was lifting and shaking the entire box-shaped classroom.

As the aftershock continued, everyone in Riku's class was evacuated to the gymnasium. The principal of the school said, over and over again, how truly lucky they were, considering that the construction crew had only recently finished retrofitting the building to make it more resistant to seismic activity. "You're all safe here now," he had said. But the concrete wall of the northern side of the school building had collapsed.

Riku was feeling dizzy, as if he were getting seasick. He couldn't tell if he was walking straight or not.

Father's cell phone couldn't be reached. The children, whose mothers came to pick them up, began to go home, looking relieved. Riku wanted to go home too, but the teachers didn't let him; he was safer here, they said, than being home alone. When Riku's father arrived to pick him up it was past six and getting dark already.

"Sorry, son." Riku's father hugged Riku and patted his head many times. "I'm so happy you're safe." He explained that his hospital was in a state of panic, and that he had gotten stuck in a huge traffic jam on the way.

And then he said, "A major earthquake has struck Tohoku."

Riku looked at his father in silence, stunned by how ghastly he appeared—as if he weren't his father.

Back home, the cupboard was toppled over, and with shards of broken glass strewn across the floor, there was no place to stand.

"We better keep our shoes on," Father said, stepping inside.

Amid the mess and chaos of the room, the two of them stood side by side and watched the TV, as it flickered with images of the same news broadcast over and over again.

In the offing of Sanriku, deep down at the bottom of the Pacific Ocean, two giant tectonic plates had clashed. The impact registered a seismic intensity of seven on the seismic scale, dealing widespread destruction across its path, all the way to Tokyo and Kanagawa. The earthquake didn't stop, though, at just shaking the land. Dragging ocean currents to the offing, it triggered huge tsunami waves that went on to rise up to forty meters high, before attacking coastal towns.

The waves, turning into roaring masses of seawater the color of lead, surged over the land, swallowing up the towns, one after another. The many who failed to escape in time drowned; a total of 15,000 lives, as a result, were lost or went missing…

To save Riku from watching the tidal waves ad nauseam, Riku's father switched the TV off with the remote. "Seems like a bad dream."

When the TV screen went blank, though, a gloomy silence enveloped the room, making Riku even more terrified.

The next day, a far more terrible thing happened; it was so terrible, in fact, that it made the whole wide world tremble in fear.

The torrential flow of the tsunami had cut off the electric power supply of a seaside nuclear power plant, including its backup supply, causing a blackout and making the nuclear reactor spiral out of control.

The nuclear reactor, with nuclear fissions occurring inside, needed to be constantly cooled with water, but the machinery was at a standstill because of the blackout. As a result, the heat generated by the nuclear fuel began to build up like a runaway train.

"We are facing a completely unforeseen challenge," said the distinguished scientists and politicians, throwing up their hands in confusion and despair. Without light, and without operational gauges, it was impossible to figure out what was happening inside the nuclear reactor. The roads were damaged by the earthquake, preventing rescue teams to reach the plant. But everyone was too afraid anyway to go near the wrecked nuclear reactor. There were even those who fled, abandoning their work.

From inside the nuclear reactor, deadly levels of radiation were leaking—levels so high a human exposed to them would drop dead like a fly. The workers there were doing all they could to restore the machinery and equipment somehow, but they made no headway at all because of the heat and radiation leakage.

Then, finally, the radioactive materials, from the nuclear reactor, began to melt. A hydrogen explosion occurred, blowing away the building. Everyone felt doomed at that moment. On the TV, words like meltdown and Level Seven Criticality flew back and forth. Scientists and experts exchanged all kinds of opinions and began to fight. But nobody really knew what was happening.

The scattered radioactive materials were carried away by the wind and spread all the way up to Tokyo, Kanagawa, and Shizuoka.

Though the Japanese government was saying that it was safe, Riku's father said, "You somehow can't trust politicians," and went on to buy a radiation dosimeter from the Internet. Still, he comforted Riku. "Don't worry, the levels aren't high enough to lose sleep over. At the hospital, we use much stronger doses of radiation for treatment, you know."

But he was the only person talking like that. Other people were very afraid of the radiation. Fearing that even Utsunomiya was going to get contaminated, everyone was panicking, and those who had relatives elsewhere, and those who became too anxious to stay, began to flee westward, clogging up the roads with their cars crammed full of luggage. It was like witnessing a massive tribal migration take place.

Only two months had passed since the disaster struck. But here they were, Riku and his father, heading straight for Minamisōma, a city located just forty kilometers away from the nuclear power plant.

Riku's father was being transferred to a new post there, as a psychiatrist in a general hospital, which was suffering a chronic shortage of physicians since the earthquake, since many of them had fled after the disaster struck. The hospital didn't really care, though, what his specialty was, just as long as he could examine the patients; they were that desperate for doctors.

Aunt Midori had said to Riku that taking a trip to Fukushima now was suicidal. Riku was far more afraid, though, of Aunt Midori's bloodshot eyes.

"Hey, everything's going to be just fine. People are still living out there, you know."

Riku's father then stepped on the gas and let the car barrel down the Tohoku Expressway while singing his favorite tune by the Beach Boys (a rock band of a long time ago, apparently).

Good, good, good, good vibrations!

Riku could tell that his father was going out of his way to lift his spirits. So, to cheer him up in return, Riku pretended to be excited about the landscape rushing past outside the window.

The ride flowed swimmingly well for a time, but the moment the car went down the Fukushima interchange and merged into the ordinary road, the radiation dosimeter, fixed on the dashboard, began beeping.

At first the two just laughed it off, with Father remarking, "What do you know! It actually works!!" Soon, however, the intervals between each beep became shorter and shorter, and in the end, the warning turned into a single sustained, continuous beep. The two looked at each other and fell silent. Father finally switched off the alarm.

A sudden hush descended inside the car.

Father abruptly said, in a steely-edged voice, "Wear a mask."

Riku removed from his backpack a mask and covered his nose and mouth with it. He then handed his father one too. At first, his father shook his head, as if to say don't mind me. But Riku continued to hold out the mask to him, so he reluctantly took it and put it on.

The car CD was now playing all Beach Boys, all the time. The breezy and sunny tunes, though, were making Riku feel all the more helpless.

Riku saw his masked face in the rearview mirror. He rarely wore a mask, not even when he caught a cold. *What a strange face...* Riku thought. *I look like a burglar.*

Flanking the road on both sides were lush meadows stretching gently into the distance, the leaves of trees dazzling in the sunlight. The dark greenery of the Tohoku region was soft and beautiful. What on earth, Riku wondered, was so dangerous about this place anyway?

It was a very nice place, so full of nature.

Even if it were contaminated, can a flimsy mask such as this really protect me? What's radiation anyway? Is it something like pollen from cedar trees?

A billboard on the roadside came into view, showing a picture of a cow. Another one had a picture of a horse; apparently there were a good number of farms in the area. But the place was empty, devoid of oncoming traffic, devoid of people.

When Riku picked up the radiation dosimeter and took a look at its digital display, the reading was rising and falling in turns. It would sometimes show three, and at other times five, and yet at other times it would drop all the way down to zero. Although Riku knew that the numbers were indicating doses of radioactive rays, he had no idea how much was high and how much was low. Without a set of criteria for understanding the figures, the numbers were, to Riku, completely meaningless.

"What's it say now?" Riku's father asked when they crossed over a mountain pass.

"Three," Riku answered.

"Three microsieverts per hour inside the car—

hmm, now that's high…" Father said, with a tinge of disappointment in his voice. But he immediately pulled himself together and—after murmuring, as if to cheer himself up, "No worries, the radiation level's supposed to be peaking out in this area"—he chewed some mint gum and floored the engine.

The beautiful forest trees, sprawling on both sides of the road, began to fly past into the distance behind father and son. Fresh green leaves, appearing all shiny and smooth, were finally beginning to bud. Spring—Riku noticed— arrives late in the northeast. He then wondered, looking up at the clear blue sky, whether radioactive materials were floating around in the vast blue there. Is the air I'm breathing now contaminated?

I can't tell at all.

If the air had an odor as strong as those air fresheners in Aunt Midori's home, I'd be able to tell and feel the fear, I guess.

After a time, the radiation level fell, and Riku's father took off his mask saying, "It's hot and stuffy." Riku, too, removed his mask and let out a sigh of relief. He still didn't get what was so frightening about radiation, though. His father hadn't even stopped him from taking off his mask; he just gave him a sideways glance and sighed, "Guess I'm human, too."

When they descended a gentle slope—after repeated ups and downs—the forest disappeared, the road leveled out, and the landscape grew familiar: gas stations, billboard ads of discount superstores, and more and more houses and stores and traffic lights came into view. But the shops were all shuttered, and not a single soul was in sight.

Riku suddenly became restless and said, "Seems like no one's around…"

Boom shaka, boom shaka, boom shaka… the music went, vanishing into the scenery.

The desolation reminded Riku of a futuristic ghost town he'd seen in a movie once. In that movie a viral infection was turning humans into zombies. They slept in dark basements during the daytime, and when night fell, they staggered outside, hungry for raw flesh. There was nobody around in the daytime world of this movie; just wild animals stalking the streets.

Riku was feeling like an action hero in such a flick. Without a soul in sight, the town, in fact, did appear as flimsy as a movie set.

The light turned red and the car stopped at the intersection. *Really?*—Riku thought—*Why bother, Dad?* Dad, however, was transfixed by what he saw beyond the windshield: a straight, grey road stretching into the distance like a strip of ribbon.

The sun was already sinking, and the sky, surging with puffy clouds, was a shiny shade of orange. Even the buildings, bathed red in the western light, were standing out in silhouette. The light turned green and the car pulled away. The high-pitched voice of the GPS guide informed that the destination was near.

"Your destination is fifty meters ahead. Voice-assisted navigation is now complete."

Turning into an alley, Riku and his father saw, standing at the end of a residential street, their new home: a brand-new, two-storied, white apartment. But even this building seemed deserted; none of the windows were draped with curtains.

"There's no sound." Riku said, getting out of the car and looking up.

"It's completely new," Riku's father said in the most cheerful voice he could muster. "And the icing on the cake is we have it all to ourselves, Riku! There were no other takers, you see, because of the nuclear accident. So I guess this place is exclusively chartered for just you and me. How do you like that?"

Riku just looked up in silence at his father. He heard him go on saying things like, you can holler all you like, or even jump up and down all you want, no one's going to complain, isn't that something? and so on and so forth. Then, like a glamorous star in a musical, with his arms outstretched, he began to sing again.

Good, good, good, good vibrations!

That day their luggage didn't arrive. Riku's father was furious and called the movers a number of times, demanding an explanation. "Well, as you know, it's an emergency, mister" was the only answer he got.

The two ate some bread they bought at a drive-in earlier in the day and went to sleep, wrapped in their sleeping bags.

"Our bags should arrive tomorrow," Father said, turning off the hanging flashlight.

Other than the occasional sound of tires made by trucks driving down the national highway, not a single sound was heard in the area. It was quiet and peaceful, with the stars clearly visible through the curtainless window.

Sleep didn't come that easily, so Riku snuggled in his sleeping bag and read Natsumi Suzuki's letter by the light of his penlight. The roundish characters of Natsumi's handwriting made him terribly nostalgic.

To Riku Sato:

I never imagined you'd ever move to Fukushima, the place where that accident happened. But your father's a doctor, so there's nothing to worry about, right? After I found out that you were leaving, I became very lonely. Do you think that's because we've been together all this time since kindergarten? And maybe also because you and I were in the same biology class, where we used to take care of Jones the rabbit? I'm going to be taking proper care of him from now on too, but he was quite attached to you, wasn't he? I'm sure he'll be missing you too. We called him "Space Alien Jones," remember? Because you used to say he's an extraterrestrial from the moon on a reconnaissance mission to Earth? Oh, I've got news for you by the way. Umm... He seems to be a she, actually.

Anyway, I'm sure Jones will be watching over you. Jones is an alien, after all.

Write to me. I'll be waiting.

Natsumi Suzuki

The Start of a New Life

The second day of moving.

Another sunny morning, the weather unusually warm for a day in May. Springing out of the sleeping bag, Riku flung open the window, through which sunlight streamed in, and cried out, "Great weather!" Then he remembered, 'Radiation!' and, while checking the expression on his father's face, closed the window quietly.

Today was the first day of school. But because the baggage hadn't arrived, there were no change of clothes. "I mean, really, what's going on?!" the father said, calling the moving company, first thing in the morning.

"Here, hold this," he said to Riku, inserting a plastic bottle of water into a camping water bottle.

"Wear a long-sleeved shirt. Don't fold up your sleeves. Got the mask? Put on your hat."

In these parts the commute to school was by school bus. Riku's father reminded Riku, "Never walk home. And, of course, no bicycle too."

Riku nodded in silence.

When the two went outside and waited in the street, a number of children began to appear and gather from alleyways here and there.

Wow! Riku thought, delighted. People actually live here after all. The kids were all wearing masks, their faces concealed behind them. When Riku's father greeted the kids with a hearty and booming, "Good morning!" they looked as if they'd seen a bear and giggled before looking up at the man and bobbing their head in response.

The bus arrived and came to a stop. It was a large minibus. When Riku stepped aboard, his father waved and struck a victory pose. *Stop it, you're embarrassing me.* Riku waved back faintly and, finding an empty seat, sat down. The kids in the bus were all sorts of ages, but they were all uniformly clad in long-sleeved shirts and trousers, their tracksuit top zipped up all the way to the neck and covering their skin. Their faces, too, were hidden behind a mask.

Clearly, Riku stood out in his clothes. It was the moving company's fault; they hadn't delivered his luggage.

Clad in cotton pants and a checked shirt over a tee-shirt, Riku was filled with regret, believing that he should have at least worn a windbreaker.

A pair of flicking, beady eyes, perched above someone's

white mask, stared Riku up and down, making him nervous, until he suddenly realized that he wasn't wearing a mask. *Oh no! Oh no! I'll get into trouble.* Panicking, he fished his mask out of his bag and strapped it on.

When he breathed now, though, his mouth turned all sticky and gross.

The bus came to a stop before the schoolyard. Everyone got off in silence, only to get sucked into the school building; in their great numbers, the swarm of masked students resembled a monster.

Riku looked for the faculty room first, just as his father had instructed him.

At the entrance there was a girl who had been on the same bus together.

When Riku asked, "Where's the faculty room?" the girl pointed down the corridor.

"Thank you," Riku said, feeling weirded out by how fuzzy and muffled his voice sounded behind his mask.

The windows of the school building were tightly shut, and even weather-stripped with cardboards. Walking down the corridor, Riku could hardly hear a thing, not even the chattering voices of any children, even though he strained his ears to hear. The place was deathly silent.

Sliding the door open to the faculty room, Riku took a peek inside.

The room looked very much like the one in his old school in Utsunomiya. Every desk was a mess, stacked with many piles of documents.

"You Sato?" said one of the teachers standing up and approaching Riku; he had a sprinkling of white hair and wore a yellowed shirt with a black sleeve protector wrapped around his arm. His face, neck, and the part of his chest that was exposed were all sunburned and brown. This teacher wasn't wearing a mask, so Riku, at the sight of his smile, felt relieved and removed his own.

"My name is Iwamoto, and I'm in charge here. Pleased to meet you." Mr. Iwamoto took Riku's hand into his, which was black and rugged as a burdock, with very stubby fingers. "So glad you came! Welcome to our school!" he continued, now tightly gripping Riku's hand with both of his, unwilling to let go. Riku felt embarrassed but was glad anyway, feeling a twinge of joy in his chest. Mr. Iwamoto's eyes were all wet and twinkly and huge, just like those of a horse Riku had seen once.

Riku decided he liked this teacher. He seemed kind and reliable.

"As you know," Mr. Iwamoto said, "our school is experiencing an emergency, and we have the students of three elementary schools all studying together here, all under one roof."

Why was it so awfully quiet then? Riku wondered. Also, why were there so few kids around?

Mr. Iwamoto said, "About three-fifths of the children, though, have been evacuated outside the prefecture."

He handed Riku a dosimeter: a thin, elongated glass badge. "Everyone in the school has one. It measures the level of radiation exposure. I'd like you to have it too."

Mr. Iwamoto fastened this tiny device, glittering like a mirror, around Riku's neck. As Riku held the mysterious object and studied it, Mr. Iwamoto gazed at Riku with a sad smile, his eyes looking apologetic, as if he'd done something wrong.

"We're going through a rough time," Mr. Iwamoto said, "but let's hang in there together, yeah?"

Riku chuckled and said, "Sure," but he had no idea what Mr. Iwamoto was talking about.

Bothered by the dosimeter around his neck, Riku kept fingering it all the time.

Although Riku had never transferred schools before, he knew what to do, having watched so many TV dramas and movies about transfer students. So he followed the teacher and entered the classroom, where he stood before his name written out on the blackboard and introduced himself, while thinking, *I sure feel like I'm in one of those stories.* He then looked around, only to find that the face of each and every one of his classmates was obscured by a mask, preventing him from telling what facial expression, if any, they were wearing.

He went on to take a seat where he was instructed to do so. The girl seated next to him was, by accident, the same girl to whom he had asked for directions to the faculty room. She had the zipper of her pink jersey zipped all the way up to her neck. Riku said, hi, but she only replied with a quick bob of her head, her shoulder-length hair parted to the side and fastened with a pin.

After the first lesson—a Japanese language class—was over, and as soon as recess began, a group of boys surrounded Riku all at once, taking him by surprise.

"Why'd you come all the way down here to Minamisōma?"

"Was your old school hit by the earthquake too?"

The boys kept bombarding him with questions, hungry for any news from outside Fukushima. Riku told them how Utsunomiya had suffered casualties, too, because of the earthquake.

"My dad decided that I had to transfer last year, on account of his work, you see."

They began to cheer him up: "Oh really!" "Wow, that must have been tough." They were all encouraging, when, to begin with, things must have been monumentally tougher for them.

Riku felt a bit relieved, though, thinking: Phew! Seems like I'm getting a warm welcome here...

But the girl seated next to him was ignoring him. She didn't even look at him, even though Riku kept stealing glances at her.

She was looking straight ahead, but her eyes didn't seem to be registering anything, giving off this eerie vibe, as if she were, in fact, a ghost. *What a strange person!*

That day, since Riku was missing many class materials, he ended up under the care of the girl in many ways.

To share a textbook together, their bodies would get close and, feeling each other's warmth, their hearts would race faster.

A refreshing wind was blowing under a May sky, the tender greenery of the plane trees outside the window swaying pleasantly in the breeze. Only if we could let that breeze into the classroom, Riku thought, how pleasant that would be.

The playground was dazzling bright in the sunlight. But there was nobody there.

The air in the classroom was stale and stuffy. It even smelled somewhat moldy. The windows were sealed up with tape.

When it was lunchtime, everyone removed their mask. Relieved, their voices also grew louder.

It was only then that Riku, for the first time, saw the true faces of his classmates, revealed in all their unveiled glory. He cast a sideways glance again at the girl next to him. This time, though, she was looking too, so their eyes locked.

(Whoa! Look at those long eyelashes!!)

Feeling his ears grow numb and warm, Riku instinctively looked the other way.

Lunch consisted of two shiso-flavored rice balls, a stick of cheese, and milk.

Mr. Iwamoto had said that, as Riku recalled, the school was using emergency food supplies for school meals. Apparently, the usual food distribution routes hadn't been restored yet.

Riku stuffed his mouth with a rice ball. It was hard and cold.

Though he longed for a decent lunch served with a bowl of steamy soup, he was still so hungry that he finished the rice ball in no time at all, and when he finished the rest of his meal he had no idea what to do next, so he looked around, wide-eyed, here and there.

Riku wanted to talk to somebody, but he couldn't find

anything to say to trigger a conversation. He had never known what it was like to be friendless. In Utsunomiya Riku used to talk with such ease, but here, he couldn't utter a sound.

There was a boy hanging around in the back of the classroom, looking tough and mean. Most of the kids were at their seat, though, their heads lost in the clouds.

After lunchtime, it was time to wear the mask again. Everybody put it on, including Riku, who, after hiding his face this time, felt comfortable. Along with his face, he had hidden his feelings too, no longer obligated to speak.

After the last class ended, Riku didn't have to help out with any extra-curricular cleaning chores; instead, he was made to board the bus—as if to be shooed away by the teacher—and go home. School seemed to be a place where you went to just study. Inside the bus there were only a few kids talking; most of the them were just sitting there, lost in thought.

The bus came to a halt at a stop designated by the school.
Everyone got off in silence. Nobody said goodbye.
Those who got off, swiftly disappeared.
I'm in a ghost bus of a ghost town.
A vacant road stretched across this grey, forsaken place.

"How was school?"
The apartment, which was now Riku's new home, had only two rooms and a large kitchen. It was roomier than it looked though.
Apparently the luggage had arrived, and Riku's father

was in the room, struggling with the PC wiring. His hospital shift was supposed to start from tomorrow.

"All right, I guess. Nothing special."

It really wasn't all that fun, Riku thought, but if he'd been honest, he would have gotten his father all worried.

"I'm hungry," Riku said, opening the refrigerator, but it was empty. His father shrugged and offered an excuse. "I went to the convenience store, but they didn't have anything to sell, so I gave up."

He then went on to mutter, "This area's still unfamiliar to me, so I'm not sure which stores are open for business…"

"Are we going to starve to death?"

"Not to worry. One thing I made sure to do was to bring along plenty of frozen potstickers."

Sure enough, the freezer was jam-packed with a well-stocked supply of frozen potstickers.

So Riku and his father ended up having for dinner, that night, some rice and a side dish of potstickers, a specialty of Utsunomiya.

After Riku polished off his dinner, he didn't have much to do other than play a video game. But he got tired of that soon enough, so he pulled out a manga book from a box and began to read.

The apartment was still littered with cardboard boxes used for moving.

Outside, it was silent, and there were no telltale signs to tell you whether it was day or night; only the clackety sounds of Riku's father typing away on the keyboard resounded throughout the room. It put Riku off from watching TV, but there wasn't anything to watch anyway, except for all those stories, streaming nonstop, about the nuclear incident.

Well, I sure picked the right time to change schools! At this rate I'll never make any friends.

Way to go Dad! You giant goofball. Why'd you have to transfer? If I were back in Utsunomiya now, it'd be after school and Yuta and I'd be riding our bicycles at top speed, racing like the wind.

Riku let out a huge sigh.

Riku had stashed away into the deepest recesses of the largest drawer of his desk, so as to hide from view as much as possible, the farewell gifts from Yuta and his friends: the kendama from Yuta, and the colored poetry card from his other classmates. The sight of those objects made him feel all fuzzy and wistful.

I never really wanted to change schools at all. I always wanted to stay in Utsunomiya, always. But if I'd told Dad that, it would have been game over for me.

Just about the only thing Riku kept handy, though, was Natsumi's letter, sandwiched between the pages of his notebook.

He remembered the rabbit hutch they took care of together, and wondered whether, today, Natsumi was cleaning the place alone, or perhaps feeding the rabbit some daikon radish leaves. They had named him Space Alien Jones, on account of his bright red eyes and long ears making him look like a being from outer space.

Remembering Jones—that rabbit white as snow—made Riku a little happy. Jones was soft and furry and warm and took to Riku very much. When Riku called him, he'd hop toward him, bouncing up and down, and munch away a stick of carrot out of his hand.

Hey Jones? Can you hear me? It's pretty rough out here you know. In fact, the inhabitants of this star are facing extinction. I seek your help.

Lost in such a reverie, Riku tossed about in bed, and gradually fell asleep.

The next day, when Riku went to school, he found the entrance soaking wet.

It was probably the PTA parents carrying out cleanup chores. But even so, the sight was strange to Riku's eyes. A cluster of moms wearing broad-brimmed hats—the kinds worn when pulling up weeds—was hosing down a concrete area.

When Riku entered, several of them called out to him, saying, "Good morning."

One of them, noticing how Riku was bewildered by the scene, mumbled, "We just want you to study without any worries, sweetie." She went on to explain that they were, in fact, decontaminating to wash away any radioactive material. She hosed and scrubbed roughly with a brush, splashing water on Riku's feet.

"I'm so sorry," she said.

"I'm… I'm okay!" Riku said, waving his hand in a hurry.

"Hey, aren't you the new student?" Everyone stopped what they were doing and looked at Riku.

When he answered, "Yes… yes," the adults exchanged glances at each other, before wearing a sad look in their eyes—the very same look Riku had seen in Mr. Iwamoto's eyes.

"What a terrible time you've come," someone's mother said, placing her hand over Riku's shoulder, her eyes wet with tears.

"Look, you're going to have a tough time in many ways, but we're here to help, so if there's anything you don't understand, don't hesitate to talk about it, okay?"

Everyone had stopped working and were nodding their heads in agreement.

"We're all in the same boat together."

"Let's help each other out and keep going, okay?"

Although Riku felt slightly embarrassed surrounded by adults, he answered, in a tiny voice, "Okay."

Though his wet socks felt icky, Riku squelched across the classroom and sat down in his seat.

Then, the girl seated next to him, who had completely ignored him yesterday, turned to face Riku and fixed her gaze on him, as if she had resolved to do so, and drew nearer.

"I'm changing schools," she said to the bewildered Riku.

"Wait, what? When?"

"Tomorrow. So, here, I want you to use this."

She handed over some supplementary materials for the class, which Riku needed but didn't have.

"You sure?" Riku asked in return. "Won't you be using them again?"

The girl kept quiet and simply faced the blackboard, wearing a stern expression. The teacher entered and commenced the morning meeting.

Riku wrote in the margin of his notebook, "Where to?"

and held it out toward the girl. The girl, after taking a quick sideways glance at the words, wrote in the margin of her notebook, "Saitama," and pushed it toward Riku.

Riku didn't need to ask why she was transferring to Saitama, because it was obvious, so all he did was write back, "Good luck." The girl nodded in silence. Since her face was partially hidden behind the mask, Riku couldn't tell what her exact reaction was like. But, if anything, she gave the impression that she was experiencing much pain.

Lunch today was fish sausage, a roll of bread and milk.

The girl, with a practiced hand, sandwiched the sausage in the roll and ate. Riku did the same, mimicking her. He was hungry, so the food tasted great. In fact, he scarfed down the meal in no time at all. The girl didn't speak to anybody. She was just moving her lips, as if chewing on something bland and tasteless.

Mr. Iwamoto said in a bright voice that, tomorrow, a number of volunteers were coming to prepare lots of delicious things.

Overjoyed, everyone applauded and cheered. The girl, too, was clapping; but apparently just to fall in line with everyone else. Riku felt sorry for her, recalling that she couldn't be here tomorrow to enjoy the yummy lunch.

The girl's transfer wasn't even mentioned during homeroom class.

Just like yesterday, as soon as the last class ended, the kids were hastily made to ride the bus.

Concerned about the girl, Riku, out of the corner of his eye, kept a close watch on her all the time. She seemed displeased, gazing sullenly out the window, still as a statue and avoiding eye contact with anyone. That look on her made her appear far older than Riku.

The bus arrived at Riku's stop, but he didn't get off.

He didn't feel like going home straightaway. Nobody's home, anyway, he reasoned.

He wanted to see what lay beyond this point down the road.

Nobody minded that Riku wasn't getting off.

So many kids are living there, Riku thought, so it must be safe.

The bus rumbled down the road from near Riku's home for another ten minutes or so before coming to a stop again.

There, the area was lined with a great number of buildings. Riku began counting, one, two, three, until he realized there were dozens of what seemed to be tenement houses, appearing run-down and overcrowded. The children, after getting off the bus, disappeared into the square boxes, as if to be sucked into them. They must be temporary dwellings, Riku thought.

His father had said that there was a residential place specially set up for people who had lost their homes to the earthquake and nuclear disaster.

The girl also got off the bus, and Riku, too, following behind the rest of the children, stepped out.

Up ahead, in a slender planter found under the eaves, a red geranium flower was in bloom, the sight of which made Riku suddenly nostalgic for his home in Utsunomiya. I can't believe that I can't return there anymore, even when it's my true home. I must be dreaming.

The entrance was littered with a tricycle and toys for playing with sand, and the laundry was hung out to dry.

The place was small and very simple, but there, wafting in the air, was the smell of life—the kind Riku had grown accustomed to. I wish we were living in this area, he thought wistfully. At least, other people actually exist here, unlike like my apartment, where you couldn't find a rat even...

"Hey there," the driver called out, snapping Riku out of his reverie. "This isn't your stop, is it?"

Aw, shoot! "I'm sorry, I seemed to have dozed off and missed my stop," Riku said, lying without intending to, his heart racing faster in fear of getting scolded. But the driver was kind, telling Riku that it was okay, and to just get back on the bus. And so Riku complied, timidly returning to his seat.

I was hoping to walk back home by myself, Riku thought, a bit disappointed that his adventure had ended in failure.

"I'll let you off on the way back, all right?"

The other remaining children were staring at Riku, eyeing him up and down, making him feel awkward and uncomfortable. *At times like this the mask sure comes in handy.*

Riku sat right behind the driver's seat, as the bus pulled out and trundled toward the sea. Yay!

Though his father had warned him not to go to the sea, Riku couldn't contain his excitement. Utsunomiya had no beaches, so Riku hadn't enjoyed that many chances to play by the sea.

The road suddenly turned bumpy. Every time the bus bounced big time, the children let out whoops of delight. Bang! Thump, thump! Yay! Wow!

"The road's rough because of the damage caused by the earthquake. You'll bite your tongue if you're not careful, so hang on tight!"

"Is the ocean over there?" Riku asked, pointing to the right side of the road. When the driver turned his head to take a look at Riku, he said, "I suppose you're not from Minamisōma, sonny?"

"Moved from Utsonomiya."

"Is that right?" The driver said, now wearing in his eyes that same look Riku had seen in the eyes of the others in this town whenever they looked at him. The driver's eyes, peering from above his mask, were like those of an elephant, all wrinkled and flabby, like the eyes of someone who had cried an awful lot.

The coastal road visible in the distance was warped like a tightly pressured clay tablet. Further beyond, a rugged wasteland spread out, the tip of which, faintly shimmering silver, was where the sea probably was.

Still as a stone, Riku fixed his gaze in the direction of the sea, noticing, in the far-off distance, sprinkled here and there, spotty patches of shadowy objects.

"They're cars—the ones that had been swept away by the tsunami and abandoned," the bus driver explained to Riku, who couldn't stop staring out the window, when he also spotted hollowed out houses that seemed haunted, and roads that seemed as if they'd been split apart by a giant man's karate chop.

(Incredible! It's like a scene in a movie)

The bus, though, instead of heading for the sea, turned right and went back toward the town.

"Don't you ever go to the seaside, understand?"

"Is it because of the radiation there?"

The driver hesitated, as if he were unsure of how to respond. "Well, no," he finally broke his silence. "It's because many folks were swallowed up over there... Some of them are probably still wandering around, unable to rest in peace."

Riku pulled back his face from the window, fearing the presences of many ghosts hovering just outside it.

All the children got off at the next stop, leaving just Riku and the driver inside. With the bus all but deserted, Riku suddenly became lonely.

A gusty breeze began to blow in from the direction of the sea.

"Around these parts here, the sea breeze gets powerful…"

With the wind lifting and whirling up the yellow dust, the landscape appeared, in Riku's eyes, like the desert.

We're all alive

The next day there was nobody seated next to Riku.

When he saw the empty seat, it felt as if the girl who had been sitting there had died.

She had left without saying goodbye to everybody.

The name, MIKA MATSUMOTO, appeared in English on the supplementary materials that the girl had given to Riku. So Mika's her name, Riku thought, tracing with his finger the blurry, felt-tip marker letters of the name.

Riku remembered his friends and his day of moving—he remembered about Yuta, Natsumi; about how everybody had written farewell messages on the colored poetry card and seen him off. When he parted from such good friends—boys and girls with whom he'd been together all the time—it was so sad he felt as if his heart was being wrung right out of him.

But here, Mika Matsumoto had disappeared. And nobody was talking about it.

It was just business as usual, as if nothing had happened, as if there never was any girl seated next to Riku, to begin with. During the final homeroom period, just prior to going home, Mr. Iwamoto finally broached the subject of Mika's transfer.

"Today, Mika Matsumoto had to switch schools because she, along with her family, had to be evacuated. Before leaving, though, she said her heart was set on returning."

There was no reaction in particular.

Not that the kids were insensitive or indifferent; it was just that they seemed to be accepting what they had no choice but to accept anyway.

Riku could imagine Mika Matsumoto getting into the car with her family, looking sad as she helped load her household effects before leaving behind that temporary housing.

She's a kindred spirit, that one; she's just like me, Riku said to himself in his mind. You hang in there, Mika Matsumoto! You be brave.

Just as Mr. Iwamoto had said, a group of volunteers arrived that day from outside the prefecture and set up a soup kitchen. It was a slightly chilly day, so the sight of the warm pork miso soup, with the steam rising, made Riku glad. Everyone moved to the kitchen in the home economics classroom to eat lunch there. Not everyone was able to enter all at once, so a long line formed down the corridor.

"There's plenty of food for seconds, so eat away, kids!!" Men and women wearing aprons were serving the food into plastic containers, one after another. "These are tough times, children, but let's hang in there, okay? Let's do our best!! We're all here to help, we've got your backs!"

Pork miso soup and *onigiri* rice balls. Riku's body started to feel warm as toast. He had two helpings in total, standing in line twice.

After the meal, commemorative photographs with the volunteers were followed by a sixth-grader's thank-you speech.

While this was Riku's first soup-kitchen experience, his classmates seemed to be no stranger to the event.

The volunteers shook hands with each child, offering words of encouragement like, "Hang in there!" It sure made Riku feel all mixed up and strange—at once happy and embarrassed, yet tense as well. This jumble of emotions had been haunting Riku all the time, ever since he'd arrived here.

There was one kid who had the cheek to say that the pork miso soup this time was only so-so.

Everyone was in far better spirits than usual, glowing with a smile on their lips, making Riku marvel at what a happy occasion it was to have people visiting from outside the prefecture. The kids were speaking louder than ever, bringing back the vitality—the life and energy—of a normal school.

The soup-kitchen crew apparently had hailed from Nagoya. Riku felt truly grateful that they had taken the trouble to travel by car from so far away to deliver all the food.

The kids lined up and saw the volunteers off, waving their hand. But after they left, everybody turned quiet again and put on their mask, one after another. Riku did the same, but was no longer so repelled by it, having become gradually accustomed to concealing his face. Riku was, in fact, rather comfortable, freed from having to expose his feelings.

Why don't supplies reach Minamisōma? Riku wondered, thinking this strange. Cars make it here, after all, so why can't we resume normal lunchtimes? I suppose we're really going through a seriously bad time. Having come from Utsunomiya, Riku couldn't wrap his head around the idea of a tsunami disaster or a nuclear power plant accident.

For the first time Riku thought, maybe Aunt Midori, after all, was right.

Riku believed the only person who would be switching schools at such an odd time halfway through the year would be him and him alone. But in the beginning of June another transfer student arrived.

It was a boy, dressed from head to toe in a brand-new blue tracksuit, which was so baggy the sleeves were covering his hands. Just like when Riku was introduced to everybody, Mr. Iwamoto wrote out the boy's name on the blackboard. Hiroki Yokota… Yes! Riku thought. A friend, at last.

During recess, Riku approached Hiroki and quietly spoke to him.

"I just switched schools, too, last month."

Hiroki looked up to see Riku's face, but no words came out of his mouth.

"I moved from Utsunomiya. What about you?"

He remained silent, refusing to answer. Just when Riku began to get anxious, though, that maybe he wasn't going to talk at all, Hiroki, in a tiny little voice, finally said, "I'm from... Futaba."

"Futaba, huh. Where's that?" Riku wasn't familiar yet with the geography of the territory around here.

Hiroki averted his gaze from Riku, looked down, and fell silent again.

The kids around them pretended to ignore their exchange. It was obvious, though, that they were transfixed and listening carefully. Hiroki didn't say anything further, so Riku quietly returned to his seat, perplexed and embarrassed.

Looks like I'm the only one who can't read between the lines.

That's the sense Riku got, judging from the vibes he was getting from his peers. Well, I've done it now, I've screwed up big time.

During dinner, Riku casually told his father, "A transfer student came today."

"Is that right? I thought you'd be the only one."

"This boy, he told me he came from Futaba."

The name Futaba seemed to ring a bell with Riku's father.

"Futaba is a town that's a whole lot closer than here to the nuclear power plant. It's completely blockaded now and all the people there were forcibly evacuated with just the clothes they happened to be wearing at the time. It's the worst place you can find yourself in today."

"They can't get back still?"

"No. It must be terrible not being able to return to your home. That boy must have been in a shelter somewhere before going on to live at a relative's house around here."

Startled, Riku froze, holding his chopsticks still. The reason why Hiroki's tracksuit was brand new, and why it was so oversized and baggy, might have been because it was from a relief agency.

Riku now regretted how thoughtless he'd been when he'd casually asked where he was from.

Come to think of it, Riku thought, when I was introduced as a transfer student everybody gathered around me to listen to my story, but today was different. Surely, the other kids must have known of Hiroki's circumstances.

Riku was lonely, feeling like a stranger through and through.

"So tell me, how's it going over there?"

Aunt Midori calls almost every day.

Riku understands that she's very worried over his well-being. But whenever Riku talks with Aunt Midori on the telephone, his head gets tense, making him feel nauseous. Aunt Midori never listens at all to his side of the story.

She only calls to confirm how correct she thinks she is, saying right away, "The radiation level is high, isn't it?"

Radiation level, radiation level, radiation level; that's all she ever talks about, radiation level!

"You can't be too careful, you know, about anything!" Speaking in a tone that seemed to suggest she knew more about Fukushima than Riku and his father, she'd say things like, "You should get a checkup that uses a whole-body counter (a device for measuring the body's internal exposure to radiation), or "Don't eat the local vegetables and meat because they're contaminated." She'd even get really nitpicky: "Wash your hands," "Gargle," "Don't dry the laundry outside—use a drying machine instead," "Make sure you always clean off the mud that get stuck to your shoes."

Every time Riku heard the word, contamination, he cringed, his chest filling with a prickly sensation; it was as though he was being sneered at, just as everybody else in this town was sneering at him. On the other hand, Riku also thought that if what Aunt Midori was saying wasn't true, Mika Matsumoto probably wouldn't have changed schools.

"What an ego you have, brother in law, to move to a contaminated area without giving a thought to Riku's welfare. At least send him back soon, won't you? You know that's the right thing to do. If something were to ever happen to Riku, why, my big sister would never forgive me."

Riku found it strange how Aunt Midori would go on and on about things she'd never seen herself, since she'd never come down here before. She really should, at least once, just to see for herself how the town was actually doing.

Lots of children remain in Fukushima today. Everyone's

healthy and carrying on with their lives. Riku didn't know the kinds of kids Auntie was talking about, either, such as kids suffering from nosebleeds so severe that the bleeding didn't stop.

But everyone was on edge, no doubt, restricted from playing freely outside, and from removing their masks without permission.

About the only significant thing that happened every day was the roundtrip journey taken between the home and the school.

To be honest it was very, very, dull—and boring, in the worst, abysmally rock-bottom sense possible of the word boring. That was the only drawback.

"Please don't worry, Midori," Riku's father says. "The situation here's not as severe as you imagine it to be."

Whenever Riku's father says don't worry, Aunt Midori's voice rises higher and higher.

"How do you expect me to stop worrying, given the situation?! The nuclear power plant remains in a critical condition, and massive amounts of contaminated water continue to drain away into the sea to this day."

Riku's father, after hanging up every time, always wears this thank-goodness look of relief on his face. "I'm fed up with what a worrywart your Aunt Midori is."

For some reason, though, this attitude annoyed Riku.

Riku's father would tell Aunt Midori not to worry.

But wasn't he actually worried himself? Wasn't he worried about the situation too? These days, he was complaining all the time, going on about how this country was the worst, or that the politicians were no good.

He'd say, "The government is clueless about what's actually happening down here—down at ground zero. Take a closer look, you damn fools!"

Riku's father had gradually become a person of this town. This upset Riku even more.

If nothing's wrong, set me free. If it's really safe, let me go play outside. You sure have it nice, don't you Dad? You're an adult after all. You can go anywhere you like with your car. But not me. There's nowhere I can go to.

If only I could get on my bike and ride. Without hardly any cars around, I'll be barreling down the roads like crazy! But it's no fun playing alone. It's boring unless I can race with all my friends.

This place is a prison.

So many mind-numbing days had piled up that Riku had become resigned to his uneventful life in Minamisōma.

He didn't want to do anything.

He thought about writing to Natsumi, but couldn't quite bring himself to do that.

Dear Natsumi, how are you? I'm doing great! Life here is fun...

Dear Natsumi, how are you? I'm not doing too well. I don't get to play outside at all..."

Riku didn't want to cry on Natsumi's shoulder; he didn't want to whine.

Although he tried a number of times to write a reply, he gave up in the end, having failed each time to put his thoughts into shape.

Before long the rainy season arrived. Damp and heavy rainfall lasted for days.

Told not to get wet as much as possible, Riku wore several layers of raincoat.

When it rained, everybody fell even more silent, muddling Riku's mind with terribly unpleasant feelings.

One month had passed since Riku transferred, but he hadn't blended in with his classmates yet.

Even though he wanted to make friends, there was no place he could interact and have exchanges. An all-out ban against outdoor activities was in place. All ball sports were discontinued, as were excursions, picnics, sketching contests; even events, one after another, were all cancelled. Everyone was also barred from staying in the gymnasium for over an hour because of the high level of radiation. Needless to say, in the case of the swimming pool, kids got warned off just by approaching it, on account of the contaminated water in there.

It had only been a month since Riku had transferred, but already four students had changed schools.

Many kids were disappearing unnoticed; none of them looked too happy either.

Riku understood that they probably didn't want to move.

Everyone's anxious, just like me.

It's such a handicap, being a kid.

Can't do anything on your own. No matter how hard things are, in the end, you have no choice but to obey the decisions made by your parents and other grownups.

During a lull in the rain, people in hazmat suits arrived

from somewhere unknown and measured, in units of dozens of centimeters, radiation levels found in the school grounds. After they took the measurements they created a distribution map that highlighted those areas where high levels of radiation were detected.

The children would avoid the dangerous spots as if those places were haunted by ghosts. This made spooky sense, especially because radiation was invisible and lingered in places, just like restligeists, those apparitions bound to specific physical locations.

At that time the adults were measuring radiation levels not only at schools, but practically everywhere else, including parks and sidewalks. They looked like ghost hunters, with their devices bearing a resemblance to poltergeist detectors.

"From now on we'll be dedicating all our resources to decontaminating the school," said Mr. Iwamoto.

For some reason Riku was reminded of the movie he had seen together with his father—Ghost Busters— and thought that a great many grownups, who were actual ghost hunters, were really going to show up. The process of decontamination involved scraping off highly contaminated soil, or washing contaminated places, or removing contaminated garbage and tree leaves. The north side of the school was shaded with so many trees that it was apparently impossible to completely decontaminate the area, so that territory became off limits.

But all the dirty soil and leaves that had been set aside by the decontamination process, though they'd been stuffed into plastic bags, couldn't be disposed of properly because there was no proper place where they could be thrown away. So they ended up being temporarily kept in some inconspicuous place. With things like rags that had been wiped clean of contamination, or long boots that had been used when walking over contaminated soil, no matter how well you separated them, in the end, you still had to dispose them at the garbage dump together with the ordinary garbage.

It was probably better to decontaminate than to not decontaminate, but it was still kind of strange, Riku thought, that no one knew what to do with all the contaminants put out. What were the grownups thinking? Wasn't there anyone among them giving some thought to the matter of radioactive waste?

Even though adults always say to kids things like, "Think before you act," they themselves needed to heed that advice.

Riku now felt that adults were surprisingly self-centered. At one time he used to believe that, unlike children, they were bright and always looked ahead. But now, he wasn't so sure anymore.

Grownups tell kids all kinds of things.

After returning from outside, don't forget to wash your hands and gargle. Hey, you've got to sweep off all the dust from your clothes, and take extra care when washing the dirt off your shoes!

But for all their talk, they themselves didn't do as much.

Grownups can't stand the sneakers kids wear; nor can they stand kids' hands.

When Riku visited his father's hospital once, he was suddenly shouted at by an old man. "Hey you!" he said, raising his walking stick to drive Riku away. "Get the hell out of here and don't come back until you've completely washed off the dirt on your shoes!"

Riku got awfully upset. What's the matter with this person? I bet he thinks all kids ever do is run around outside like dogs. What a joke! We're not even allowed to step outside, let alone run around.

The old man, wearing a gloomy look on his face, kept mumbling to himself while remaining seated all the time on the bench in the waiting room.

All sorts of people were there, including this one man standing before the elementary school building, staging a *kamishibai* picture-story show that told the story, through terribly scary picture slides, of how bad for your health radiation was.

There were even those who had come from the city and were bowing and apologizing to children, saying things like, "I'm sorry we've turned this world into such a terrible place."

Such adults annoyed Riku very much, making him go, Yeah, okay, whatever! Just let me play, all right? It's super dull and boring around here; there's nothing to do.

When the rainy season finally ended, it turned July and the scorching weather arrived.

The temperature rose and rose.

Windows weren't allowed to be opened, so, boy, was it crazy hot! The three electric fans whirling in the classroom were just churning blasts of hot air.

Riku's father got angry, shouting, "Why the hell can't they install air conditioners in the school?"

Riku couldn't tell who on earth his father was getting mad at. Whenever Riku came into contact with such grownup rage, Riku's body would get all tense, before he tried to calm his father down, in such instances, by behaving cheerfully. But such perseverance on Riku's part didn't last for long. Adults were angry all the time, after all. Adults were complaining all the time, after all. Adults were vindictive, after all.

Riku was tired. But so were all the other children; everyone was dead tired.

The number of brawls went up in the classroom. The causes were trivial: *You said so—No I didn't; You took it—No I didn't...* Once sparks flew, feelings exploded. And since letting off some steam, especially under these circumstances, led to relaxing stress relief, everyone gradually began to enthusiastically look for chances to explode. Riku, as the new kid, though, kept a low profile to stay aloof and harmless. Even so, his personal things, like his pencils and erasers, would disappear now and then, before he knew it. And every time when his stuff went missing like that, Riku felt sad while thinking, To hell with it.

Riku suddenly flew into a rage when someone tapped his head with a rolled up sheet of exam paper that was handed out. Usually, Riku would just say, "Hey, that hurt," and laugh it off, but this time he turned all serious and looked sullen and glared at the offender, who also glared back at him. Riku thought, I don't want to do this, but I'm still mad. "What you lookin' at?" "What'd you say to me?" A punch is thrown in the air, carelessly. Riku, too, throws one back in return. Before Riku knows it, he's engaged in a serious scuffle. Summoned by the teacher, Riku and the other kid get scolded and the two shed tears. So who's to blame? Nobody, really. It's just that they were both pent up with frustration.

When summer arrived, the town was said to be increasingly running out of its power supply, so the key thing the people had to do was save electricity, save electricity, and, by all means, on a city-wide level, save electricity. Save Electricity had become Minamisōma's catchphrase, with public announcements being broadcast every day, such as, "Let's restrain the use of air conditioners; "We request all citizens to cooperate to achieve sustainable energy consumption."

Amid the boiling heat, the classroom remained tightly sealed.

It was hot as hot could be. The children were perspiring so much that even the desks and the floor got wet and sticky with their sweat. A foul stench, like the smell of something rotting, was also floating in the air, causing some kids to feel sick during class. The grownups feared that it was due to radiation. But with such scorching weather, Riku thought, couldn't it be that the kids were just suffering heat strokes?

Even though it was summer, some protective parents insisted on having their kids still wear nothing but long sleeves and long trousers.

Nonetheless, at that time, the clothes began to vary.

Some kids still wore a mask, while others didn't anymore. Riku's father said, "Don't bother, it's safe," so, Riku, too, thought the same, just like the other children, surely.

Twisted around the little fingers of parents, kids who claimed that masks were useless clashed against those who claimed that it would be dangerous without them. Dangerous! Safe!—they'd argue back and forth before the argument would erupt into a full-fledged fight. But truth be told, nobody knew anything.

During recess, no child ever stepped outside. Nobody ever did.

The idea that the playground was dangerous was a commonly held belief; Avoid going outside as much as possible; Don't get exposed to radiation.

School, in this way, was a ginormous prison.

In a corner of the playground was seen a steady pileup of deep blue plastic bags, which contained topsoil that had been scraped off in the decontamination process. The blue was reflecting in the sunlight so vividly it was eerie.

The area around the pile of plastic bags, cordoned off by a rope slung between stakes driven into the ground, was also off-limits. This begged the question: Did decontamination make any difference when all you ended up doing was pile up radioactive waste like that? That's what the children thought anyway, but no one dared to speak.

Grownups. What they did was a total mystery.

When the atmosphere got too suffocating to bear, Riku began to take refuge in the shade of the gymnasium's storage shed, where the air was cool.

Since he had been told not to approach the trees, Riku chose this shed instead. It stood removed in an otherwise empty space, where a nice wind blew in from the sea. Of course, Riku was told that exposure to the wind, too, wasn't a good idea, but…

Going outside was Riku's little rebellion.

If it were so dangerous, why were people still living here? Wasn't that odd?

The weather was so fine that the blue of the plastic bags and the blue of the sky were blending into each other.

Riku, hugging his knees on the ground, was gazing up at a lone lamb-shaped cloud floating above, when he heard someone say, "Now that's a really nice breeze, don't you think?"

Turning around, Riku saw that it was Mr. Iwamoto. When the teacher took a look inside the gymnasium's storage shed, he said, "Oh great!" and proceeded to pull out a small bench from inside and place it under the eaves. Then, after sitting down with some effort, he tapped the bench to signal to Riku to come and sit next to him.

"Before the accident," Mr. Iwamoto began, "all the children used to play in the playground. The town is blessed with a rich natural environment, so life in this land used to be really comfortable and pleasant…"

Even now, though, as Riku scanned his eyes around the area, the birds were happily singing on treetops, a swarm of butterflies were fluttering about, the greenery of the mountains had grown even thicker than before, ants were crawling on the ground, and spiders were spreading their webs. The only ones afraid of radiation, it seemed to Riku, were humans.

"I don't think it's a good idea to get too worked up, but then again, nobody has ever experienced the kind of disaster we have."

The glass dosimeter was hanging down from Mr. Iwamoto's neck as well, glittering in the sunlight.

Riku asked what had been on his mind all this time: "Does radiation really have an impact? I mean, is it true that if you absorb lots of radiation, you could wind up with cancer in the future?"

Mr. Iwamoto stretched while letting out a prolonged Ummmm, before finally saying, as the bone in the nape of his neck—from bending his neck—went crack, crack, "Well, that's a difficult question. In Japan, they say one in three people die from cancer. I'll probably get into trouble with the parents for saying what I'm about to tell you, so this stays just between you and me, but the truth is, nobody really understands what the impact of radiation is. Sure, some say there's an impact... but nobody really knows. And you can't do anything about what you don't know anything about, can you? But there's one thing you can say for sure. We're all alive here, today, aren't we? This is an absolutely unmistakable truth, isn't it?"

"...Uh-huh."

When Mr. Iwamoto, with his darkly tanned face, laughed, his white teeth twinkled in the light. Up close, Riku saw that Mr. Iwamoto's wrinkles ran very deep, as if they'd been chiseled into his face.

"Nobody knows anything about tomorrow. Not even those great scientists; they certainly couldn't predict the earthquake and the nuclear accident—so what's the use of worrying? No good can come of it. And that's why I say we should all just carry on with our lives without any worries, even though that may be a little reckless. Peace of mind, after all, is far better than worrying."

"Really?"

"Sure, my great-grandfather used to say that. He lived to be a hundred years old."

"Wow, that's amazing!"

Riku, who was still only ten, found such an ancient age mind-boggling.

"I come from a long line of livestock and agricultural farmers who've been making a living out of this land, but the tsunami has washed all that away, along with the house."

Riku learned then, for the first time, that Mr. Iwamoto's parents' home used to be in the danger zone, close to the nuclear power plant, and that Mr. Iwamoto, too, was a victim.

"Back at my parents' place, we were raising three heads of cattle. When the accident occurred, though, we were told not to take along any animals kept within the 20-mile radius of the nuclear power plant, so we left our cows behind. Many creatures were left to their fate. Cows, horses, dogs, cats, chickens... I surely feel sorry for them. It was a terrible thing we did."

Riku, without thinking, asked, "Did they have names?"

"Names? You mean the cows?"

Riku nodded.

"Well they're not pets, you know," Mr. Iwamoto said, laughing uneasily. "Come to think of it, though, there was this one cow who became very attached to me, and so he ended up becoming the only one I actually did name."

"What was his name?"

Mr. Iwamoto mumbled shyly, "Baytaro… He appears in my dreams sometimes, poor guy."

Listening to Mr. Iwamoto's story, Riku was reminded of Space Alien Jones, the white rabbit he used to take care of together with Natsumi.

"I used to look after a rabbit myself, as a keeper."

"Oh yeah? You like animals?"

"Yes, I like animals."

"Did this rabbit of yours have a name?

"…Space Alien Jones."

"Jones, huh!" Mr. Iwamoto said, laughing.

"But it seems he was a she."

The Lonely Space Alien

In the summer of the year the accident happened, various associations and companies stepped up to invite the children of Fukushima to destinations outside the prefecture, including overseas destinations. In fact, some children were even invited, along with their family, to Italy and Hawaii.

"Riku, why don't you take a trip this summer? There seems to be all sorts of educational camps for children... and I think all the kids living in Fukushima are eligible to join."

Despite such encouragement from his father, Riku didn't feel that motivated. He was, after all, feeling a little apathetic about all kinds of things these days, shrugging them off with a "whatever" attitude all the time. For this reason, he wasn't up to facing any new challenges.

"I don't want to go by myself," Riku said, knowing fully

well that his father couldn't leave here.

As expected, Riku's father began to look very apologetic and troubled. "I'd like nothing more than to accompany you, son, but that'll be difficult to do this year."

The hospital is experiencing a serious labor shortage. The entire staff were evacuated to places outside the prefecture, so those of us left behind have to divide various workloads among ourselves. Even after you go to sleep, Riku, your father stays up till late in the house, sitting at the computer.

In the end, with Aunt Midori insisting, or rather, steamrolling, the decision was made to send Riku away in the summer to Aunt Midori's house in Yokohama.

Even though Riku wasn't enthusiastic at all—not one little bit—his father and Aunt Midori had fixed his summer plans for him without his say so. Surely, Riku thought, Dad was more comfortable without me around.

Riku's father drove Riku from Minamisōma to Fukushima station.

It was the first time, for Riku, to ride the Shinkansen bullet train. Riku reached the ticket gate and raised his hand and said, "So long," but after that, he never turned back to look at his father. He couldn't hide his bubbling anger. These days, his shoulders were always tense and his head hurt all the time. Even though it was summer vacation, he felt dull and halfhearted.

The Tohoku Shinkansen took just a little over one and a half hours to reach Tokyo. The journey was so rapid it was disappointing.

Aunt Midori was waiting at the platform of Tokyo Station.

As soon as she spotted him she rushed over and said, "Oh thank goodness, it's really wonderful to see you safe and sound," and hugged Riku. As expected she smelled of air fresheners. Even though she'd said it was the fragrance of herbs, the smell, to Riku, was so grassy and strange it turned his tongue bitter.

Tokyo Station was thronged with families on their summer vacation. Riku felt dizzy at the sight of such a frightfully massive number of people. Everybody was in a hurry; plenty of souvenir shops everywhere; there was a small child, lost and crying; there was a man dressed in a suit gliding past this child, wearing a scary look on his face; there was a woman with arms and legs so long—like a fashion model's—it took her a great deal of effort to walk without bumping into others.

Riku was also surprised to see that there weren't that many people wearing masks. It was a whole new world, where nothing seemed to have happened, neither the earthquake nor the nuclear disaster. *What is this place?*

Aunt Midori was happy to see how overwhelmed Riku was by the city.

"See? It's safe here, right?" she kept saying over and over.

Once they arrived at the apartment in Yokohama, the first thing Aunt Midori did was to take Riku to the bathroom, where she said, "Remove all your clothes and take a shower immediately."

Wait, what? Why? Riku thought, but he did as he was told.

I guess she wants me to take a bath because she thinks I must be sweaty. But I did change my underwear before leaving.

When Riku finished bathing himself thoroughly and stepped out of the shower, his clothes were already tumbling round and round in the washing machine.

Aunt Midori was standing before this machine, her hands in plastic gloves. All of Riku's things, including his shoes and rucksack, were put inside a transparent plastic bag. This made Riku uneasy, as if something was tightly squeezing a part of him deep inside his chest. Aunt Midori smiled and laughed and placed new underwear, clothes, and socks into a basket and handed it over to Riku, saying, "Here you go."

"Give me back my things!"

"Don't you worry," she said, raising one hand up. "I'll return them to you if, after measuring the radiation level, I don't find anything wrong, so be a little patient, okay?"

Having said that, she went and fetched a dosimeter, opened the plastic bag, and plunged the gauge into it. With every reading that appeared, she shrieked, "I knew it! It's high!"

From the back of the corridor, Riku's two cousins were peering in his direction with fear in their eyes.

"What do you mean by high?" Riku asked.

"I mean not normal."

Riku, clad in the baggy bathrobe that he had been made to wear, attempted to snatch back his belongings from his aunt's hand.

"Get your hands off, bad boy! These things need to be

decontaminated."

"Back in Fukushima, us kids were carrying on fine with all our stuff."

"Oh. My. God," Riku's aunt said, her face turning into Munch's Scream. "I can't believe it. What on earth is the Japanese government doing? Every single child in Fukushima needs to be evacuated. The government must set up schools with dormitories attached so that the children can study in safe environments. It's incumbent upon Japan to do so, being an advanced nation."

Aunt Midori wiped with sanitary wipes every single item Riku had brought along with him, including his pencil case, pencils, and even textbooks, and after she was done, she threw away those wipes into a plastic garbage bag before sealing it tight.

Akane came out and picked up Riku's textbook between her thumb and fingertips and took a sniff.

"Hmm. Radiation has no smell, eh?"

"Stop nosing around," Aunt Midori scolded Akane. "Get back to your room and stay there!"

Akane stuck her tongue out and fled. Takuto, on the other hand, was looking at Riku with an expression that said, 'How regrettable.'

When all her work was done Aunt Midori looked satisfied and turned to Riku with a smile on her face. "You can relax now."

Isn't that what you should be telling yourself, Aunt Midori? Riku thought.

Even during dinner she kept saying, "All the ingredients

I use are nothing but safe ingredients, so I want you to relax and eat to your heart's content, all right? You've got nothing to worry about now."

Takuto and Akane were frequently stealing sideways glances at Riku, who was just sitting there with his side dish uneaten, though his chopsticks were touching the food on the dish.

Riku's uncle, while munching away the "safe food", asked with wonder, "So what on earth do you eat when you're in Minamisōma?"

"At school, a group of relief workers come over and prepare lunch for us. At home, Father cooks and we eat ordinary meals."

"Ordinary meals?" Aunt Midori probes.

"Umm, like frozen potstickers…"

"Oh, good, that' safe."

"You know, you say ordinary," the uncle said, "but you're living only—what—thirty, forty kilometers away from the nuclear power plant? I can't believe human beings still live there."

And then, after discussing for a while how poor the state of Japanese energy policy was, the bespectacled civil engineer concluded with the assertion that the nation nonetheless needed to go on relying on nuclear power generation for the sake of economic development. But Aunt Midori lashed out, "You're still talking such nonsense. Nuclear power should never be used again, ever!" Their argument got nowhere and abruptly ended when Riku's uncle fled the scene.

On the first day Takuto and Akane asked Riku to kindly

not touch their personal belongings.

Riku could tell, from the look in their eyes, that this request wasn't made out of any nastiness on their part, but out of genuine fear. It figures, Riku thought, they've been subjected, day after day, after all, to the things the "Board of Education" has been telling them.

Riku slept alone in the living room, on a futon laid out for him there.

For the first time he missed Minamisōma. Have I become someone who belongs there? No, that' can't be. I'm different from the people who've been living there all their lives. When I'm in Minamisōma, I hate seeing those gloomy-faced grownups with their masks on. But on the other hand, here in Yokohama, I hate seeing grownups like Aunt Midori, who cower in fear all the time, telling me over and over, it's dangerous, it's dangerous. I don't belong in either places; not in Minamisōma, not in Yokohama.

Lying on the futon, by the sofa ensemble, which was apparently made in Sweden, Riku stared at the palm of his hand. We're all alive... huh.

Riku began to feel that, ever since the earthquake, he'd been sleeping in unfamiliar places all the time.

The next day it was decided that Riku and Takuto would go swimming at the city-run pool.

Aunt Midori showed the dosimeter to Takuto and convinced him that Riku's reading showed a "safe value."

"See? Even contaminated materials can become safe, as long as they're properly decontaminated."

"That's right, Takuto. No worries," Riku said, before

embracing Takuto on purpose and roaring with laughter when Takuto got upset. While laughing, though, Riku became scared; he felt as if somebody else in some distant place, instead of him, was laughing derisively with a sneer.

Takuto wasn't a mean-spirited person, so Riku knew that, as long as he persuaded him with reason, he wouldn't be unsympathetic to Riku. But, still, he seemed to be utterly clueless to what Riku's life was like back in Fukushima.

"Hey Riku, is it true that in Fukushima insects have become, like, gigantic?"

"Yeah, we've got ginormous mutant grasshoppers and beetles creeping and crawling all over the place there."

"Wow! Seriously?" Takuto said, his eyes lighting up brilliantly at Riku's words.

"Of course not, you twit!"

"Oh, bummer…"

Remembering how Riku himself had, when he'd arrived at Minamisōma for the first time, been reminded of, at the desolate sight of the uninhabited town, a science fiction movie, he let out a sigh, seeing that he used to be no different than Takuto in his thinking.

"But radiation levels are high right?"

"At my school in Minamisōma, simply approaching the swimming pool could get you scolded… because it's supposed to be contaminated."

Riku was falling into despair, waiting for the train at the platform of a futuristic subway station. He now understood that it was absolutely impossible to make Takuto understand the reality of Minamisōma. All he—and everybody else around here—saw were the statistics.

And you couldn't understand anything from just numbers. It'd be good if everyone were to just visit once... if they did, they'd all see what was really going on; they'd know, for a fact, that we were all carrying on with our lives…

"Hey Riku, can you see the nuclear power plant from your home?"

"Are you kidding me? The answer's no."

"Oh, okay. Hey Riku, do you always hang that thing around your neck?"

Takuto glanced at the glass dosimeter.

"Yeah, it measures annual exposure, I'm told."

Takuto said, "So you're something like a guinea pig."

Riku felt extremely uneasy, as if he had just stepped on a pile of doggy doo in the street. But he couldn't put a finger on exactly what made him feel that way.

"I have to keep this around my neck because the grownups are afraid of radiation. They shovel off contaminated soil and stuff it into blue plastic bags and drop them off nearby, here and there."

"But what's the difference, if they put all that soil nearby?"

"I know, right? Honestly, I really don't quite understand myself what adults do. But they're all doing their best, so us kids, we're, like, just going along with whatever they do."

Takuto sighed. "Ahhhh… dude, I tell you it's tough satisfying grownups."

Riku thought that it was very strange for him to be right here right now. He felt all alone, as alone as a lone space alien on Earth could be.

The pool, too, was teeming with people. In fact, there were so many people that, rather than humans, they seemed more like a school of fish. Why in the world were there so many people? Back in my apartment my father and I were still the only residents there.

Everyone looks happy. They're not afraid of anything. They're in high spirits, so full of life, and enjoying summer. The air conditioner's blowing at full blast. Even the use of electricity here's limitless; it's all you can consume.

When I was living in Utsunomiya I never felt Utsunomiya and Yokohama were that different from each other.

But coming to Yokohama from Minamisōma, I find everything's different. Too different.

It's like another planet here, Jones.

Sitting at the edge of the swimming pool, dipping his feet into the water, Riku couldn't get his mind off Minamisōma.

The blue bottom of the pool reminded him of the blue plastic bags containing decontaminated things.

"Ah come on, aren't you going to swim?" Takuto said, elegantly breast-stroking his way toward Riku.

Once he reached him, though, he lifted his head from the water and whispered, "Listen, do me a favor. See those kids over there? They're friends of mine. Now, whatever you do, never tell them you're from Fukushima, got it?"

At that moment Riku was about to say, in a knee-jerk reaction, that he wasn't a Fukushima kid.

But he didn't. The faces of Riku's classmates in Minamisōma burst into his mind. Standing up, his head reeled and the sounds of people having fun in the pool became suddenly distant.

"You going home, Riku?"

Riku ignored Takuto calling out to him, and began to walk away. After taking a shower he scrubbed his body vigorously.

Damn it... he muttered.

All I did was change schools. I didn't want to, but I did it for Dad's sake. But the next thing I know I've become something other than what I was before.

Riku was at a loss. It seemed like he had transformed into a zombie unawares, and this frightened him.

I wonder if zombies know they've changed into zombies. Or do they forget who they used to be?

They forget. Yeah, I'm sure they do. That's why they, like, attack family and friends.

So am I the same Riku Sato as before, back when I used to live in Utsunomiya?

Riku returned to Minamisōma one week earlier than planned.

I have to get back; I can't stand it here anymore, Riku had cried involuntarily over the telephone until his father finally gave in and said, "I understand, I understand."

When Riku got into his father's car at Fukushima station, Riku sulked and pretended to fall asleep. He didn't want to speak to his father all that much. His father too, in turn, didn't wish to say anything to Riku, not with the way he was behaving. The two remained silent all the way home.

Even though Riku had come back to Minamisōma because he'd missed his father, when he came face to face with him Riku became, for some reason, extremely annoyed.

"Did anything happen at Aunt Midori's place?"

"Not really, nothing in particular."

Riku's father shrugged and pretended to be unconcerned.

Good, good, good, good vibrations. Riku saw that his singing father's heart was heavy with sadness. Surely, Riku thought, he must be thinking about what Mom would have said at a time like this.

Riku had come to gradually know his father's mind. Which was why it was even more difficult now for him to stay a good boy.

I can tell that you're suffering, Dad. You always look bright and happy but you don't fool me. It's obvious.

Riku's father was looking sidelong at Riku, who felt his father's eyes on his back while gazing out the window.

A fluffy cloud, white as snow, was floating in the sky... when, from somewhere, Riku heard his mother's voice calling out, Riku, hang in there. Then, in the rift between the clouds, her face faded into view. Riku suddenly felt all alone again.

Throughout the summer break, all Riku did was laze around at home and sleep. Even though his father encouraged him to go outside and play sometimes, Riku refused and stayed put, saying, "No way, I'll get contaminated." Decontamination operations were, in fact, already underway in many places, but radiation levels in

Minamisōma remained patchily high.

Riku's father checked radiation levels every day. But in front of Riku he wore a look that said he couldn't care less. This irritated Riku even more.

A nuclear power plant stood just a stone's throw away.

Restoration of the damaged nuclear reactors was nowhere in sight.

Readings of radiation levels appeared in the newspapers every day, just like the weather forecast.

There was no news that could brighten the day.

Hospitals were still short of helping hands.

Riku gathered that no doctors or nurses were willing to come to Fukushima.

Riku's father would come home at midnight, all worn out and exhausted.

The only stories Riku heard lately, spreading virally from mouth to mouth of all sorts of people, were those that told of malicious deeds: someone played a prank on a car that had a Fukushima license plate; someone was prohibited from entering a restaurant the moment it came to light that he or she was from Fukushima, and other such tales.

Although the grownups pretended to be fine, they were actually very anxious and scared.

Riku felt this sharply.

He wanted to cheer up his father, who was working so hard, and Mr. Iwamoto, who was so kind. But there was something like a dark poison steadily pouring into Riku's heart, robbing him of his strength.

Every time the Internet or the weekly magazines reported on the health hazards of radiation, the telephone assault from Aunt Midori would begin, devastating Riku and his father with her blasts of extreme worry rays.

"I get so worried I can't sleep at night you know!"

"Look, what you read in the weeklies are absolute rubbish. I work at a hospital, and I know for a fact that in this area, only one person has been reported to have fallen ill from radiation exposure."

"So what? What about five years from now? Can you tell what the future will be like five years from now, can you? Listen to me, it's not right. How can you even allow yourself to raise a child in a high-risk area?"

Riku's father hung up violently.

"Oh for goodness' sake," he said, "she should just come down here, at least once, and see for herself!"

Lying on his side on the tatami mat, reading a manga book, Riku stole a glance at his father's face. He was like a bear these days, walking back and forth around the house and chewing mint gum.

Then, Riku noticed a square patch of sky framed in the window, and thought, Dad, you don't even open the window that much anymore, not ever since we moved to Minamisōma. You used to open it even in the winter, telling me that the air would get stuffy if you didn't.

So, for all your talk, you're afraid of the radiation, too, aren't you Dad? You're actually upset, aren't you Dad, of being told the truth by Aunt Midori. Maybe it's just that you don't want to admit what a mistake it was to have moved to Fukushima.

Riku's head was a mess; it was as though his mind was being blackened out with a permanent marker.

I give up, he said, sighing and rolling over.

The tatami mat's damp. The air's stuffy. How long are we going to go on living like this?

This sucks…

Before he knew it, Riku had lost himself inside the darkness of a ghost town. In this darkness were found, aimlessly wandering around, zombies who had lost their souls who, given the chance, would gnaw away at Riku. All alone now, Riku felt he had no choice but to stay put indoors and keep safe.

Riku began having fewer and fewer conversations with his father. The second semester had begun, but all he ever did each day—still—was to go to school and come back home. Riku couldn't get motivated for anything. Many relief volunteers would offer encouragement, but when they said things like, Hold on, or Keep on keeping on, Riku would get even more heavy-hearted. Still, he'd give a smile anyway, since they expected one.

Say cheese!

It was such a hassle having to go along with the empty pep and gusto of the grownups. It sapped Riku's strength even more. It disgusted him. It made him weary. Whenever Riku lay down on the tatami mat to play games, the next thing he knew, the day would be over.

The Riku of those Utsunomiya days had vanished.

There was nothing he could do about what he'd become.

2

INTO THE KINGDOM OF WHITE

"Hello, Mr. Nomura!!" the children said in unison, bowing their heads. Mr. Nomura looked round-eyed at them and said, "What well-mannered boys and girls you are!" Above his thick eyebrows were snow crystals piled up like lumps of sugar.

"It's terrific to see all of you, thank you for coming."

He hugged each and every child, but when he reached Riku, the last one, he just stood before him, paused, and said "Hmmm" while gazing at him intently, before joyfully breaking his stony expression.

"I look forward to working with you," Mr. Nomura said and, unlike the way he greeted the other children, he gave Riku's right hand a strong grip and stared into his eyes.

Riku was flustered and, after skipping a beat, gripped back in return, saying, "I look forward too."

Why did this person stare at me?

Although mystified, Riku was nonetheless glad he'd received special treatment.

In this homestay program, Riku, a fifth grader, was the oldest, or in other words, the leader. In all, five kids were going to stay, for five days, at Mr. Nomura's house: the first-grader Masato; the second-grader Chaco; the third-grader Seyla; and the fourth-grader Ryo. They were all standing in the snow with bright-red cheeks and sparkling eyes, when Mrs. Nomura called out, "Come quickly, come in, come in. Cold, isn't it?" and began to usher everyone from behind. She was round like a ball, and her movements and voice were springy and bouncy like one too.

Mr. Nomura's home was a very old and huge mansion, smelling of a good old bonfire. The doorway—a spacious earthen floor—was chilly and dim. When the children were told to take off their shoes there, they all scrambled to get in first, except Riku. He stayed behind and neatly arranged their boots, which were strewn all over the place, before stepping onto the floor where a white reflection of Riku's face appeared on its polished shiny black surface.

A screen depicting a landscape—the kind that appears in historical dramas—was there, and beyond this screen, in the back, a large fireplace.

Firewood was burning in the hearth. An orange kerosene lamp was lit. The scene was like something out of a movie made a long, long time ago.

"Wow! Look, it's a bear, it's a bear!!"

The children, in their excitement, couldn't stop patting the stuffed bear in the *tokonoma* alcove. Hey, come on, you can't touch without permission—Riku was terrified as he grabbed hold of Masato who was horsing around.

"Uncle, is this real?"

Mr. Nomura patted Masato's head and said, "Of course it's real."

Next to the bear, perched on the branch of a tree, was

a stuffed eagle. Below that was a stuffing of a fox-like, yellow-furred animal. "This fellow here's a marten," Mr. Nomura said. "You can usually find one in a mountain. My great-grandfather caught it."

The sight of the rigid animals made Riku feel slightly unpleasant—I wonder if those glass-bead eyes shifted back and forth at night.

The children, led by Mr. Nomura, streamed deeper into the dim-lit mansion. Just how many rooms does this place have anyway? In one room there was a display of a magnificent yoroi armor helmet, and in another, a Japanese *katana* sword.

Seriously, this place is haunted...

After being led down an endless, zigzagging corridor, the children were shown into a six-tatami room with a partition and told to set down their luggage there.

"After you put down your bags let's all have snacks, okay?" All the kids said, "Yes, Mrs. Nomura!!"

Surprised, Mrs. Nomura involuntarily raised her shoulders and said, "My, my, how lively!"

The children had been strictly taught by the staff that they needed to greet their hosts with respect and properly reply when spoken to, and that, because they were going to be under the care of other people, they had to be polite without exception.

This was the first homestay experience for Riku; he had never stayed in the house of someone he'd never met before. At first, though, Riku felt that he wasn't up to taking a tour, that it was too much trouble. But he changed his mind the moment he heard his father remark, "The destination is Hokkaido."

"Hokkaido? So that means, like, there'll be snow?"

"Soft and fluffy powder snow, just sitting there waiting for you, dude!"

Billed as a chance to encounter nature, the tours were scheduled to run during the summer, winter, and spring breaks. Any child residing in Fukushima was eligible to sign up.

Remember your good friend in Utsunomiya? Yuta? Well, his mother was the one who told me about this tour, Riku's father had said.

"I tell you, Mr. Sato, this Fukushima Kids Project is apparently very good, and there's much talk about it on the Internet too. They even have a program for the winter. Why not get Riku to sign up?"

When Riku's father read this email he had a hunch that, if the program was about Hokkaido in the wintertime, Riku would show interest.

So one day Riku's father, while wearing a smirk on his face, came over to Riku and whispered into his ear, "About that winter vacation this year…?"

Riku promptly turned the other way and sulked, seeing that his father was about to flatter him.

Ugh, so hokey, these grownups…

In the past, the sight of his father's smile alone would make Riku all bubbly and happy, but now that very same smile kept him on his toes, making him dread what on earth was going on in his father's mind.

He's probably trying to get me to go along with some

other scheme of his again. Just like the way he got me to move here.

Riku had begun to believe that all his bad feelings he'd been having lately was because of his father's transfer.

I'm never going to trust the things he says anymore.

"This hands-on nature tour has all sorts of programs, you know. Look, there's even one featuring a trek through snowy mountains. Sounds like fun, don't you think?"

Snow, huh. Suddenly, Riku's mother's face floated into view.

(Riku, don't trouble your father too much, okay?)

Startled, Riku reluctantly decided to look at the pamphlet with his father.

Turning the page, oodles of pictures appeared, showing children playing by the sea, in the forest, and by the river. They were all so cheery and sunny it made Riku envious. Why do they look so happy?

Riku's father was silent. When Riku casually turned to see him, though, he was snuffling.

"What's the matter, Dad?"

"Well… the faces of these children—they're deeply touching, aren't they? They make me feel all tingly inside… and remind me of how much you too, Riku, have been wanting to go outside and play…"

Riku was stunned, seeing how moved to tears his father was.

Dad has been worrying about me in his own dad kind of way, I guess… It wasn't that he was too absorbed in his work to give a hoot about me—about whether I was around or not. It wasn't anything like that at all.

Riku, too, felt a stinging sensation in the back of his nose and, bit by bit, verged on tears.

Actually, I knew how you really felt, Dad. But I was, like, annoyed and taking it all out on you.

Sorry, Dad.

Still, Riku couldn't get thrilled anymore, not in the same way he used to before, when, by now, he'd be innocently jumping up and down and shouting, "I want to go! I want to go!" But he did feel like going to Hokkaido anyway. It was, after all, a place of memories for Riku's family of, formerly, three.

"Well, if you insist, I guess I could take the trip just to get you off my back."

"Great! That's settled then."

Riku's father held Riku's head in his arms, and the scent of disinfectants from the hospital—the scent of his father—coursed through Riku's nose for the first time in a long time.

I feel a bit tricked, but I'm touched; Dad still thinks of me.

And so Riku signed up for a six-day-five-night nature tour and homestay program.

The night before departure Riku got so excited he didn't sleep a wink.

Wow! All that snow heaped up there. Imagine that.

Hokkaido was the destination of the final trip Riku took with his father and mother, when his family still numbered three.

Mom used to love the smell of the snow in Hokkaido.

I'm going to that pure white kingdom again.

The first day was orientation day.

Everyone stayed at a large, hotel-like establishment found inside a quasi-national park in Onuma, Hokkaido.

In all, two hundred children, from various places throughout Fukushima, were jostling each other in the assembly hall. Riku, who hadn't traveled outside of Fukushima in a long while, was on edge, having been nervous throughout the long journey to Hokkaido.

These kids are all Fukushima kids. But not me. I'm different. Am I even allowed to be here?

Filled with such hesitation, Riku tried as much as he could to stay under the radar.

The itinerary of the program was jam-packed with so many events that there was no time to relax and take it easy.

"It sure was a long trip, wasn't it?" one of the staff members said. "Thank you for coming all this way! Now, before we do anything else, let's just get outside and move our bodies!"

The moment the children set their luggage down they headed for the world of pure-white snow outside.

Play, play, and—whatever you do—play away!!

The volunteer staff took the lead by rolling over in the snow, leaving all the children, at first, just standing there, stunned.

"Is it really okay to play?" one of them asked aloud.

The kids looked at each other before making up their

minds: "All right then, let's go!"

When a snowball flew into his face, Riku's heart, which had been closed until then, opened up all at once as he remembered his naughty, mischief-making Utsunomiya days.

So it's really okay to run, right? I'm allowed to roll around, right? To touch anything as much as I like, right?

Even the trees, even the ground, even the snow. And, if I want to, I can even eat the snow, right?

I'm free!! I'm free!!!

Playing in the snow. Having snowball fights, making a snowman, it was all so much fun; the kids were all strangers to each other, but because they were, they were opening up to each other all the more quickly.

It wasn't just all play, though. The children, in solidarity with the staff, would prepare meals and clean up afterwards as well.

The local mothers taking care of them—who would say, "Thank you all! You're all so responsible!"—were all friendly and kind.

"How good of you to come, thank you!" many others would also say. "Thank you for coming?" Riku thought. To the contrary, we're the ones who should be saying thank you.

After dinner was the nightly meeting. The older boys and girls, who were among the staff in charge of guiding the kids, were all so cool and stylish, each in their own way. Riku could see that they were dedicated to helping the children, and, along the way, being so full of life themselves, to having their own fun too.

They didn't say a word about what scary things might be in store for the future, or whether they were afraid of radiation; they didn't even complain or express doubts about society and politics. What's more, they didn't even feel sorry for the children, never saying things like, hang in there. They treated everybody on equal terms.

Riku felt as though he'd come across, for the first time in a long time, truly lively and cheerful grownups.

With such adults no kid would ever have to be on his toes, losing his mind over whether he's being troublesome or not.

"Okay, listen up now! When you say yes to someone, say so in a clear and loud voice. Make sure you properly say thank you, excuse me, I'm sorry, thank you for the delicious meal, good morning, good night, and other greetings. Be punctual. Keep your promises. Be courteous. After using the restroom and bath, be sure to put back every item used to where they were originally found. Always keep your hands clean—mind you, this is not for yourself; this is to ensure that you don't spoil the home of your host. Always stand in the other person's shoes before you take action. Understand?"

Riku, who had never stayed overnight at someone else's home, except those of his relatives and friends, became doubtful whether he could stay polite in some stranger's home arranged by a homestay program. After all, when he had borrowed the restroom back in the homes of his relatives or friends, he had always left the washstand wet, and never even bothered to neatly rearrange the restroom slippers.

I've got to get my act together.

Riku felt as if he'd suddenly turned into an adult himself.

Riku was the oldest anyway. He had to take care of kids younger than himself. There was Ryo in the fourth grade; Seyla in the third; Chaco in the second; and Masato in the first. All of them were younger than him. For Riku, an only child, he had gained, in these kids, for the first time, his very own younger brothers and sisters.

"Okay everybody. Let's have a blast for five days!"

"Yeah!!"

On the day of departure, at Onuma Station, one of the staff, an older brother type, grabbed a hold of Riku's shoulder and said, "You're in charge now."

Passing through the human archway created by the staff, the children boarded the train, and as they did, Seyla was singing "10,000 Feet Up in the Alps", Ryo was brushing away the hands of the human archway, Masato had gone to the toilet just prior to leaving and was still missing, Chaco was hanging in midair, dangling down from the human archway. Here, everything turned into play. If it didn't, it felt like such a waste.

But this is the way it should be, this is what's natural...

Riku began to feel strange, as if his days in Minamisōma were nothing but a long nightmare.

They were now on their way to somebody's home in the foothills of the Komagatake volcano in Hokkaido, where just the kids—the five of them—would spend four nights. The staff, after seeing them off, would head back, leaving everything in the hands of Riku, the leader. Glancing at the four naughty children, and pondering the huge responsibility that had been suddenly thrust upon him, Riku let out a sigh.

I wonder if I can handle it. I wonder what kind of person Mr. Nomura is. I hope he's kind.

That day Komagatake was hit by a snowstorm. When they boarded the microbus, which had come to pick them up, a gust of snow blew their way, causing everyone to holler in terror; someone even cried, "We're going to get lost and never be found!"

It was so white outside the window that Riku wondered, as his heart began to race faster, whether they would all reach their destination safely, with the wind howling, and the visibility zero.

Ryo spooked Chaco, "The snow fairy's going to come out!" Seyla chimed in with an in-your-face authority, "There might be a yeti out there too!"

When Riku wiped the steamy window with his gloved hands, a world of pure white appeared, bringing back memories of his mother. In the snow, Riku felt, the presence of his mother still remained. Motionless, he fixed his gaze outside.

Father, Mother… Riku was searching inside his heart for his family. It was as if the Riku of many years ago—the little Riku who had, once upon a time, come here on a ski trip together with his family—had woken up and was beginning to stir back to life.

"This area here, children, is the area of a very fine

mountain named Komagatake, or Ezo Komagatake, as it's also known. By tomorrow the snowstorm should blow over, so let's all head for the mountain then. You'll find a wonderful array of animals there, so it's going to be great fun."

While listening to Mr. Nomura tell his story, the children were seated around the fireplace eating buttered potatoes. Mr. Nomura appeared to be around sixty years old and was dressed in a black jacket and tracksuit. He was skinny and didn't have that much of that much height. His hair was black, but considerably mingled with grey strands, and he grew a mustache and a beard just around his chin. His eyebrows were very thick and below them were remarkable, double-fold eyes, whose irises, Riku thought, glittered gold sometimes, compelling Riku to look closely into Mr. Nomura's face.

Riku had never seen eyes like that—Why is the color of this person's eyes so mysterious?

On the first day after dinner, the children took turns to take a bath, and were in bed by half past nine.

Time flew while clearing the table, washing up, spreading the futon, changing into pajamas, brushing teeth…

The younger kids made a noisy fuss about how creepy the restroom at the end of the dark corridor was.

It was a tiled stall with an old-fashioned wooden door. Although it did look a bit spooky, the toilet inside was a Western style one and its seat was warm too. On the floor, by where your feet would be, was a small electric heater even.

When Ryo, with his arms drooping down and his eyes wide open, bellowed, "Woooooo… I'm going to eat you all!!" Masato and Chaco screamed and ran out into the corridor. Hey, hey, we have to be quiet. By the time Riku caught the small children and made them finally go to sleep in their futon, it was already past ten o'clock.

Riku, as the last one up, turned off the lights, and slipped under his futon cover. Moments later, the shoji door slid open.

It seemed to be Mrs. Nomura checking in on the kids. After she slid the shoji door shut again, the rest was silence, except for the sounds of the night outside, moaning and roaring.

The futon smelled of herbs. It was heavier than the futon back home, reminding Riku that he was in a brand new environment, a place he was visiting for the first time in his life, a place where he didn't have to wear any mask.

Riku took a deep breath and exhaled slowly. At long last, a sense of calm had been restored; he felt, as he used to once before, peaceful and easy enough to be able to take long, leisurely, deep breaths, which he now took again and again in the dark.

Every time he took a deep breath he felt the tension in his body slipping away.

The weather next morning was bright and clear. The snowstorm had completely passed.

Leaning out the sash-window of the porch, the children all shouted in chorus, "Wow! Beautiful!!" A world of silver enveloped the garden, the tall trees, the short trees, completely covered in snow.

"One yeti, two yetis, three yetis…" Masato said, starting to count the trees.

"Four yetis… that's a lot of yetis!!"

So many, many yetis, he said, running about the living room. "Hey! You must keep quiet and behave yourself," Seyla rebuked. "Whoa, I'm scared!" Ryo said, making fun of her. Chaco, on the other hand, was doing as she pleased, lying down all the time, blasé to all the tomfoolery.

After going to the kitchen and washing his face, Riku smelled the comforting aroma of miso soup. Inside a large dining room was arranged a huge tatami-room table laid with meals.

This house is so huge, Riku thought, I wonder if it's just the two of them—Mr. Nomura and Mrs. Nomura— living here. No sooner had Riku had this thought than he noticed, for the first time, a thin young man in glasses seated at the far end of the tatami-room table. His hair was all rough and knotty, apparently from a night of tossing and turning in sleep. When his eyes met Riku's he nodded lightly, prompting Riku to nod back in panic.

The young man, along with everybody else, expressed gratitude for his meal, saying "itadakimasu," and began to eat. Well, he must be someone living here after all, Riku thought, but when Riku looked away only for a moment, he was gone, as though he had vanished into thin air. Riku became uneasy, wondering whether there had been any young man there at all.

Riku said, "Hey guys, you know that person who was

just there...?" Ryo said, "Huh? What are you talking about? I didn't see anybody there."

"You're kidding. But I saw somebody—a thin man wearing glasses."

"I knew it! This place is haunted," said Chaco.

Surely, in such an old house as this, it's easy to imagine a ghost or two might be be wandering about, but, honestly, come on. Mr. Nomura, who had been listening to this exchange, said in a subdued voice, "That's my son, Yoichi. He's studying for the bar exam."

Oh good, he was real, Riku thought, feeling relieved. "Bar exam?"

"That's right. He tells me he wants to become a lawyer. He's been unemployed, though, for two years already, and I have no idea how much longer it's going to take."

After breakfast Masato and Chaco began to play in the snow. Riku, too, stepped out into the garden and grabbed a heap of pure white snow and tried to harden it into a ball but he couldn't because it was too powdery.

Wow! That's pretty... they're like gemstones, Riku marveled, gazing at the snow dazzling in the sunlight, when a snowball, without a warning, thumped into him. It was Ryo.

"All right you, you're asking for it now."

"Ha, ha!"

The two of them began to roll all over the place, smearing each other with snow.

Seyla said, "Let's make a snow cave."

Everyone helped out and built a snow cave by hardening

the snow, but later on, after everyone entered the narrow space inside, it became jam-packed and quickly collapsed. Seyla exploded, yelling, "It broke because you're rough, Ryo!" Ryo put on an innocent air, while Chaco and Masato began to build a snowman.

"Ryo, you blockhead!" Seyla continued. "You're a meany."

Riku was at a loss, standing beside the sobbing Seyla. Girls sure have a rough time…

Mr. Nomura came and showed the kids a pair of snowshoes. He said that they were woven out of straws by an acquaintance of his.

Mr. Nomura said, "These days, you don't see that many artisans like my friend anymore who weave with such fine craftsmanship."

"Wow, what's this, what's this?" Seyla said excitedly, having already bounced back.

Everyone began learning how to use the snowshoes, which looked like giant sandals. Mr. Nomura attached them to his feet and began to walk in them.

"There's an art to snowshoeing," he said while demonstrating.

"You turn both your feet in this way, see, and walk like a courtesan." Ryo asked, "What's a courtesan?" Riku answered, "A geisha girl in the olden days. I've seen one on TV before; a woman of the Edo era, wearing heavy makeup and walking in really tall wooden clogs."

Mr. Nomura said, "The snow is deep. You can't walk in the mountain without snowshoes. So practice well, you hear?"

"Yeees!" they all answered enthusiastically, but before long, most got tired and ended up returning to the house with Mrs. Nomura.

Only Riku remained, standing there, filled with wonder at how remarkably near the distant mountain felt, now that the place had fallen silent after everyone had disappeared—the whistling wind was blowing past over the snow; great white clouds were drifting across the sky, veiling the sun sometimes, before, once again, through breaks in the clouds, the sun would reappear.

Sparkle, dazzle, sparkle, dazzle... The scenery's all so brilliantly white—how pristine it is, how divine it is. Riku tried taking a deep breath again. The air was so refreshing it was like peppermint.

Walk like a courtesan, Riku reminded himself, as he practiced over and over. But he just couldn't get the hang of it; every time he tried his foot would just sink into the snow at once.

Damn it...! This is harder than I thought.

A considerably large and empty field stretched before Mr. Nomura's house. But underneath all the snow piled up over the ground, this clearing might as well have been a plowed field, or even a rice paddy. Over this completely flat bed of snow, Riku continued to snowshoe. He'd just take a few steps, and his foot would sink, going SLOSH! And when he'd try walking again; SLOSH! But in the course of practicing again and again, he gradually began to get the hang of it and walk for long stretches at a time.

Okay, I'm getting good at this now.

Delighted, he went on snowshoeing, leaving behind a zigzagging pattern of footprints, his field of vision nothing but pure white snow now. In time, he felt as though he was floating in white, as though he were swimming deep inside a world of purely pristine white.

Feels so good!

Riku plopped down on the snow and lay there sprawled.

This is super awesome!

He closed his eyes, tasted freedom, and opened his eyes again, only to see this time, though, Mr. Nomura's face before him. Surprised, Riku jumped to his feet.

Mr. Nomura, looking at Riku's footprints, seemed impressed and told him, "You've been trying really hard, I can see… and it looks like you've done it; you've mastered the art of walking in snowshoes!"

"Yes, well, somehow."

"Good. In that case, you're ready for some mountain trekking. Do you like mountains?"

"When I was little I used to often go skiing with my parents."

"Is that right? Well then, have you ever hiked up a real mountain?"

A real mountain? What's that? Riku shook his head.

Mr. Nomura gazed at the sky and listened to the sound of the wind.

"The wind's going to start blowing a little in the afternoon today. Let's try leaving tomorrow afternoon."

Wait, what? Can this person talk to the wind? No way.

It didn't escape Riku's notice that, when Mr. Nomura looked up at the sky, his eyes glittered golden again.

The Secret Incident

Oh no! Riku thought.

He had woken up yet again around two, just as he regularly did, feeling sort of itchy and restless and sour, wanting to pee and not wanting to pee at the same time. Before long he'd get to the point where he really wanted to pee until it became so unbearable he just had to get up and go.

The night of the second day. Riku made sure to answer nature's call before going to sleep, but he still woke up anyway. Staring at the black planking of the ceiling, Riku became even more disappointed, thinking, Ahhh... this isn't home.

What to do? It's cold, and to reach the toilet of this old house, I have to walk down a dark and endless corridor.

Now that seems really scary to do in the dead of night.

Riku tried to suppress his urge to pee but it was no use.

Getting up reluctantly, Riku tiptoed between the futons so as to elude the notice of Masato and Chaco and the other kids, who were all fast asleep, breathing peacefully. Masato, though, had made such a racket before slipping into his futon, but the moment he lay down he fell asleep in no time at all. Chaco was even more of a sleepy head. She already seemed drowsy when she finished her meal— We all played a lot, didn't we? Riku thought, feeling so close to the younger children, now that they had become as endearing as his own family.

He slid open the sliding paper-fusuma-door and stepped out into the corridor. The soles of his feet felt chilly as Riku heard the shutters rattling. The wind outside must be gusty, Riku guessed, convinced that, after night fell, this house became creepier and creepier. Even the beams were creaking, and, once in a while, they also made a popping sound like when a tree splits apart.

On the way to the toilet, after turning a corner in the corridor, perched on its branch was a stuffed hawk with its wings spread out. The mounted animal's perfectly round eyes were giving Riku the shivers, as they seemed to be glaring at him—I really don't want to pass by this bird so late at night.

The darkness of this corridor was already spooky enough—the darkness that seemed alive, rustling and squirming with all sorts of unspeakable creepy crawlies.

The hawk was looking Riku's way, so he rushed past it to avoid eye contact, when a loud bang came resounding from the toilet in the back.

Ahhhhh! he cried, unawares, before taking a pratfall.

A small shadow jumped out of the depths of the lavatory. Riku blinked. What the hell was that? A rat?

The old wooden door slid open with a creak.

"Whoa!"

"Sorry about that, guess I scared you, didn't I?"

It was the young man in the glasses.

"Ah, um, um, um…"

Unable to stand up, Riku couldn't form a coherent thought.

"You want to go to the toilet, right? Here, I'll accompany you… so you don't have to be afraid, okay?"

Shaking his head at the hand stretched out before him, Riku stood up in a flurry and said, "Tha-that's okay. I'm good."

The young man chuckled. "I'll just wait for you here, so you can relax, okay?"

Riku felt so much at ease that he was on the verge of tears. When he rushed into the toilet room—a lavatory dimly lit by a single light bulb dangling from the ceiling—and finished his business in a jiffy, he washed his hands in a great hurry. The young man, wearing a large sleeveless *kimono* jacket with a scarf around his neck, was standing in front of the washroom. "Wait, slippers!" Riku remembered, and returned to the toilet room and carefully aligned the direction of the slippers before bolting back to the young man.

"What a well-brought-up boy you are! Well done!"

The young man looked into Riku's face, impressed. Riku

felt slightly proud; it felt like he had been praised on behalf of all the children.

Riku was still tense, though, when the young man leaned in and whispered into his ear, "Hey, I'm going to have a cup of hot chocolate now. What do you say you and me enjoy some together?"

Hot chocolate!?

Riku's face glowed at these words. But won't I get scolded if I did something like that so late at night, without the other kids?

"Not a word to everyone else. It'll be our little secret," the young man said, finger on lips.

Without a second thought, Riku nodded, realizing that this would be his first time, ever since his mother had passed away, to drink hot chocolate, his special favorite.

The young man removed a can of powdered cocoa from the top of the shelf in the kitchen, and warmed some milk from the refrigerator in a pan and made the cocoa dissolve little by little. Ahh, that sweet old smell; sure brings back memories. The old home in Utsunomiya was coming back to life again--the kitchen where Mom was; the smile that Mom wore.

The young man carefully stirred the simmering cocoa with a spoon, gently clinking the pan. Then the young man led Riku into his study, and there, by a warm kerosene heater, Riku slurped hot chocolate. The drink was warm, and so sweet that Riku felt his heart tighten.

"You know, even I used to be afraid to go to the restroom at night when I was a child."

"Really?"

"You see, back when my great-grandfather was still alive, I'd heard that the tonchi was spotted in the house."

"The tonchi?"

"Yeah. Apparently it's a tiny sprite standing at a height of just around twenty centimeters. I never saw one myself, but my father said he'd seen the tonchi."

The small shadow that had jumped out of the lavatory flashed across Riku's mind.

"Is that like an elf?"

"Who knows. I'm really not sure. Apparently the tonchi has been around since ancient times. My great-grandfather used to say that the tonchi is an incarnation of the mountain god, who protects the house. My family comes from a long line of arboreal artisans who cultivate trees in the mountain. We cultivate saplings until they turn into huge trees and then sell them. We wait for dozens of years, you know, until they become straight and tall. But today the number of such artisans has dwindled down to just a handful few; not many these days have the endurance to persevere in such painstaking work. In my family's case, the tradition ended with my father."

From above the ceiling the pitter-patter of something running across resounded. The two looked at each other.

"Nah, it can't be..." Yoichi said, looking up. Riku, too, following Yoichi's line of sight, looked up.

What kind of creature is the tonchi? And what does he mean by the family tradition ending with his father?

Thinking it rude to ask, Riku kept quiet and continued to sip his hot chocolate.

The desktop of the young man was stacked with thick

tomes filled with nothing but difficult kanji characters.

"Does God really exist?"

"Can't say. But the people of this land believe so. The tonchi's supposed to be a good-natured fellow, giving gifts and even helping humans cheer up."

Wondering if the tonchi was walking around nearby, Riku, without intending to, cast a sidelong glance at a corner of the room.

"By the way, what's your name?"

"I'm Riku Sato. The character for Riku is the same as the character for land."

Riku had answered in a loud voice, so, when it occurred to him that it was late at night, he covered his mouth in a panic.

"I see. That's a good name. "My name is Yoichi Nomura. The Yo in Yoichi is the character for *yo* in *taiheiyo*, the Pacific Ocean. So you see, you and me together, why, we're land and sea!"

Land and sea! Riku nodded with great pleasure, suddenly realizing his own name was pretty cool.

"What do you dream about becoming in the future?"
"Umm, I'm not sure yet."

"Of course not, why would you be, you're still only in the fifth grade." Getting a faraway look in his eyes, Yoichi laughed forlornly.

"Why did you think about becoming a lawyer?"

"Because I want to help people. The law's a very complicated thing, so if you don't know anything about it, you can suffer huge losses or become disadvantaged, or at times, even be taken for a fool and swindled. But nobody reads law books, right?—not if you're leading a normal life. And that's why, when you're in trouble, you need an expert you can rely on. Don't you agree?"

"Yes I do."

"From now on, many people in Fukushima are likely going to file lawsuits. I hope I can be of help to them someday."

While listening to Yoichi speak, Riku was thinking about his father.

Come to think of it, Dad had said something similar before we moved to Minamisōma.

He'd said that there are people in trouble in Minamisōma, that in times of trouble, people with specialized knowledge become necessary, and that if he could be of help, even in a small way, he thought he ought to travel to Minamisōma.

Dad at that time was really cool. Of course, that's not to say that he wasn't anymore, but something was different.

"Okay, tomorrow's an early day again, isn't it? You should get to bed already."

Yoichi saw Riku off to the children's room, and, after making sure that Riku had tucked himself into the futon, he quietly closed the sliding paper-door.

Under the heavy futon cover, Riku continued to relish the lingering aftertaste of the secret, late-night cup of hot chocolate. That's right, Riku thought, it was a secret. My secret, and mine alone.

There appeared, in the darkness, without a warning, his mother's face.

(Good for you, Riku)

Yes, Mama. The people here are all very good.

Warmed by the hot chocolate, Riku fell asleep at once.

A tight sensation on his stomach awakened Riku—someone was stepping on it.

Owwww… Riku said as he saw Masato's foot hovering over his face. Then, still groggy with sleep, Riku cried, "Tonchi!" and got up.

"Tonchi? What's that?" Masato said, throwing his arms around Riku's neck.

Even Chaco and Ryo had already woken up and changed clothes. Seyla was facing a mirror in the adjacent room, getting dressed. Riku looked at the clock in a panic; it was still five minutes before wake-up time.

Safe, Riku thought sighing, and, while still sitting on the futon, he slipped into his pants, wondering if yesterday's incident was all just a dream. But the faint flavor of cocoa, still remaining in his mouth, was unmistakable.

"Yes! Today's going to be a bright and beautiful day too!" Riku said stretching, when a pillow hit him on the head—bonk!

"Ah, hell!" Riku said, instinctively throwing back the pillow and triggering an all-out, raging pillow war throughout the room.

"Breakfast is served," came the voice of Mr. Nomura from behind the paper door. But when it slid open, somebody's pillow flew into Mr. Nomura's face, bringing the battle to an end as everyone froze in their tracks. Mr. Nomura, though, just smiled, laughed, and, while rubbing his forehead, said, "Okay then, how about some war games outside today! Just you wait. I'll be sure to settle this score."

When Riku rolled up and put away the futon and washed his face in a hurry and went to the hall, preparations for the meals were already underway. It was a great feast; so great in fact it seemed too extravagant for a morning meal.

All the children helped serve the meals together; Seyla and Chaco poured tea from large kettles into teacups; Ryo and Masato carried bowls of miso soup very carefully so as not to spill any on the way; Riku was in charge of setting the chopsticks and bowls on the table.

Let's see now, the chopsticks should be arranged so that the sides you hold point to the right, and the rice bowl goes to the left of the miso soup bowl, just so.

Mrs. Nomura was in high spirits today as well, hustling back and forth from the kitchen, when there appeared, from the back of the kitchen, two elderly women with steaming boiled potatoes.

"Good morning everybody! So wonderful to see you all here. Now come and have some freshly boiled potatoes!"

They were apparently neighbors; a duo made up of a chubby auntie and a scrawny auntie.

"Oh for goodness sake," the scrawny auntie said, "do you really think the children would want to eat potatoes in the morning?"

"Why, of course they would. You do love potatoes, don't you children?"

"Yes we love potatoes," the children all said in chorus.

"You see!" The chubby auntie said, happy as a clam.

"It's absolutely marvelous with buttered soy sauce, so bon appétit, my dears, enjoy to your heart's content!" The scrawny auntie said, spreading plenty of the butter, which smelled so good.

Before arriving in Hokkaido, Riku never thought he'd receive such a warm welcome from the people here. It was rumored among the children, after all, that kids from Fukushima would get bullied.

Even if you were a transfer student, if it came to light that you were from Fukushima, you'd be left out; They'd even throw out the kids' belongings, you know—that's how afraid they are of contamination. Such snippets of conversation among the parents would reach the ears of the children and, like weeds overgrowing in gardens, darken their hearts.

They're just going to feel sorry for us, that's all, Riku thought. Just like at Aunt Midori's place, they're bound to undress us and check our radiation levels.

When Riku was welcomed with huge smiles and the words, "So thrilled you came!" by a large number of the staff at the pickup point, he felt as if a heavy load, which he'd been burdened with for so long now, had been swiftly lifted.

Nobody there was taking pity on him, with worry creasing their forehead. Instead, they'd simply said, "Let's play together."

Looking at their sunny smiles, Riku was on the verge tears, fully understanding, right there and then, that his heart had been weary all this time, that before he'd known it, he'd become terribly sad and gloomy.

It had been only three days since he'd arrived, but Riku was already feeling bright and cheerful, freed from the mental pressure that was weighing his heart down. It was as if he'd grown wings, even. Breathing was comfortable too—Come to think of it, I used to always wake up feeling like this back when I was in Utsunomiya. Wow! I'd forgotten.

After the children cleared the table and tidied up their baggage, it was decided that they would all hit the road to the mountain. Riku intended to shepherd the small kids into the restroom and answer nature's call himself before returning to his room.

Trying to catch up with everyone, Riku was in a hurry when he noticed that a sliding paper-door facing the corridor was open, probably for cleaning. This house really has a lot of rooms, Riku thought. But no sooner had he passed this door than he caught, from the corner of his eye, something flashing by. Surprised, Riku froze in his tracks.

Anyone there?

Riku backtracked and took a peep inside the room.

Hanging on the walls enclosing the square, dark room, were old photographs.

Lured by the mysterious atmosphere, Riku set foot inside, where the scent of incense lingered in the air and the tatami felt chilly.

The photographs were those of many dignified faces, all looking down at Riku. He stared back at them one by one. There was a man sporting a mustache; a *kimono-clad* woman with her hair put up; a man in military uniform— In which era were these photographs taken? They were all yellowed. The people in them seemed important-looking too; could they be the ancestors of Mr. Nomura's family?

Wait, is that the great-grandfather who built the stuffed bear? Before he knew it, Riku was snickering. The thick, centipede-like eyebrows were just like those of Mr. Nomura.

The photographs gradually became newer, changing from monochrome to color; the times, Riku understood, were advancing toward the present.

His heart went thump, though, when he saw, hanging at the furthest end, a photograph in mint condition of a boy of around Riku's age.

It was as if he had seen a picture that wasn't meant for his eyes.

The boy was laughing, his fingers forming the peace sign, his lips a little like Yoichi's.

He was the only child in this photo gallery. Was he dead?

Shuddering, Riku quietly edged back and left the dark room.

Mr. Nomura came over, bringing along scads of snowshoes.

He told the children that he had his friend make enough for all of them.

After Riku helped the small children wear the snowshoes, they all went wobbling together outside, where the snow, reflecting the sunlight, was shining silver. It was so dazzling, in fact, that everybody squinted.

In the morning they snowshoed through the forest near the house.

Walking clumsily—scrunch, scrunch—the children—over the fresh bed of virgin snow that had yet to be marred by footprints—left behind theirs in all directions.

"The ground around a tree isn't firm, so don't get close to it—you'll fall."

The moment these words left Mr. Nomura's lips a child fell through the snow with a loud thud, causing everyone to panic and rush to help the buried tot. Only those areas surrounding the trees had cavities of almost a meter, over which if you walked, you fell through instantly. But, frankly, this was fun. It was so much fun, in fact, that everyone fell into them on purpose, going wild with excitement and bubbling with laughter. Sooner or later, though, lump after lump of snow from the trees would fall suddenly. When this happened, Ryo performed the role of an ascetic meditating under a waterfall to tremendous cheers and applause.

Seyla and Chaco created a lot of small snowmen, arranging them like *jizos*, the guardian deities of children, and placing before them offerings of snow dumplings. The snow was so dry that if you patted your jacket the snow would scatter like powder in the air and dance down twinkling.

Riku was already snowshoeing masterfully over the snow.

"Well done, Riku! You've become really good at this!"

Praised by Mr. Nomura, Riku was super happy.

"All right then, why don't you and me, after lunch, set off together for the mountain."

Riku was surprised. Apparently Mr. Nomura was

inviting only Riku to the mountain with him.

"The little kids can't possibly go yet, you know. But you, Riku, you'll be all right, and I'd really like to show you my mountain."

Riku felt his heart throb at the thought of just the two of them traveling to the mountain. Is this, Riku wondered, what it feels like when you go out on a date with a girl?

That day, in the afternoon, they headed for the mountain in Mr. Nomura's large, four-wheel drive.

Riku, who was sitting in the passenger seat, was clueless as to where and in what direction the vehicle was running. All around all he saw was a snowy world of silver, the sky, as if iron pressed, a stiff, ghastly shade of pale without a speck of cloud in sight, the wind a mild breeze.

The Animals of the White Kingdom

"Okay, from here we walk."

Stepping out of the car, they put on their snowshoes. Inside Riku's rucksack were hot drinks and rice balls and, in addition, some sweets and chocolate bars. Mrs. Nomura let them bring along these goodies.

"Well, have you attached your snowshoes properly? Let me see."

While having his knot fixed, Riku gazed at the round back of Mr. Nomura who was stooped down before him. It was smaller—Riku thought, surprised—than it appeared to be when Mr. Nomura was standing up.

"Okay then," he said rising to his feet. "Let's go."

Riku answered, "Yes" and followed him, seeing that, by

then, Mr. Nomura had become the same old Mr. Nomura.

The word, "Yes," is an amazing word, Riku thought.

When you say, "Yes," your heart gets jolted to the core with a solid boost of energy.

Come to think of it, back at school, even at home for that matter, I never reply properly. I'd often just answer half-heartedly or unwillingly, going, "Yeeesss" or "Yeah, yeah" or "Alright already."

But now that I'm here in Hokkaido saying "Yes" all the time, with all the pep and gusto I could muster, I have to say, it feels great.

It was as if his heart was starting to shine, and this made Riku glad.

Mr. Nomura's gait, as he made his way up the snowy mountain, was limber.

He was moving his body slowly to the right and left, advancing smoothly just like a skater. Riku on the other hand was awkward, quickly losing his footing to the slushy snow. What's more, there was no rustling coming from Mr. Nomura. He was extremely quiet; not at all like Riku, whose clothes would rustle every time he walked; even his rucksack would go squeak, squeak.

Why can Mr. Nomura walk so quietly? He's just like a ninja.

Riku desperately tried to keep up with him, but he soon fell behind. The more he hurried the more entangled his feet got. Calm down, Riku tried to tell himself, stick to your own pace and walk carefully.

"Are you all right?"

"Yes sir! I'm fine."

"You kids really know how to reply properly, don't you? It's refreshing."

Taking one cautious step after another into the snow, Riku finally caught up with the back of Mr. Nomura, his steamy breath glittering and sparkling like dancing diamonds.

"Hey Riku, take a look at this. What do you think this is?" On the bed of snow were footprints of a small animal continuing all the way to the end of a gently sloping white hill.

"A rabbit?"

"That's right. Well done!"

A pleasant breeze blew across.

"I was the keeper of a rabbit in my previous school."

"This is a hare. It just might be nearby."

Mr. Nomura swept his eyes over the area.

On the snowy slope was the shadow of a tree, which, to Riku's eyes, appeared like a person dancing without a care in the world, his arms and legs outstretched in wild abandon.

"Do you think rabbits are playing around outside today too, because, like, the weather's so fine?"

After Riku said this, Mr. Nomura paused a little before saying, "Rabbits aren't humans. They don't play."

When Riku, in response, then asked thoughtlessly, "You mean rabbits don't play, like, at all?" Mr. Nomura looked at Riku and, in a no-nonsense, clear-cut, even coldhearted, tone, said, "For rabbits, survival is everything. They don't engage in an activity such as play." Riku decided to stop asking any further questions.

Instead, he recalled Space Alien Jones, who used to keep still in his hutch.

What was Jones thinking of all the time?

Just then Riku had an epiphany; it was as though he saw, for the first time in his life, the world through Jones's red eyes: the dull grey rope; the shadow of a human approaching to feed him.

Jones often used to kick the soil with his hind legs, as if to be tapping out a rhythm. Natsumi used to laugh, calling it the Jones Dance, but now that Riku thought about it, he wasn't so sure anymore if that was a dance.

After a while Mr. Nomura stopped walking.

He looked back in silence, a finger to his lips, having spotted something, apparently. He pointed to the space between the two trees to the right.

And then Riku saw it—a small creature on the snow, glittering in a golden hue.

Riku's heart thumped, skipping a beat.

"It's a marten," Mr. Nomura said. "Don't let its' tiny size fool you, though. This animal's a ferocious predator."

A marten!

Transfixed, Riku trained his eyes on the creature.

What beautiful fur! The tail, bushy and golden and shiny. Sensing the presence of humans, apparently, the marten lifted its face and was quietly looking Riku's way. The head and tail were white and the feet were black, as though the marten were wearing socks. The appearance was comical, yet the animal gave off a seriously ferocious vibe.

Even though they were standing a 100 meters apart, Riku—who also seemed to be under a hypnotic spell, standing there motionless like the creature—could feel the jittery tension of the marten in all its vibrant glory. Shrinking back two, three steps, the marten smoothly changed direction and demonstrated a magnificent jump, as if to fly across the sky, freed from gravity, while drawing a perfect arc in the air, swooping from right to left before disappearing into the depths of the forest. The movement was so flawless the marten's entire body seemed to be made of muscle. It was so awesome to see.

"That was amazing!" Riku said, sighing, when Mr. Nomura said, "The marten's fur fetches a high price, so it's been overhunted; I'm afraid the natural enemy of the the marten is us humans."

Riku, who had never in his life encountered a wild animal, was overcome with an adrenaline rush. It was as if the wild energy of the marten had transferred into his body.

"You're lucky, you know," Mr. Nomura said, gently stroking Riku's head. "The chances of spotting this animal are rare."

In the snow Mr. Nomura's eyes assumed an even more golden hue that it was scary.

"What's the matter?"

"Your eyes, they're golden, aren't they?"

"Ah yeah..." Mr. Nomura said, looking radiant. "Must be because I got snow-tanned."

Thereafter the two sat on a sunlit snowy incline and ate onigiri rice balls in pristine silence.

The snow seemed to be absorbing all sound. Minamisōma was also very quiet, but the silence here was different. It was a rich silence—a golden silence, even; the kind that made you feel it was okay for two people to stay quiet all the time, the kind that didn't need words.

After finishing the rice balls, Riku wanted to ask so many questions, but it felt like something was going to break if he spoke, so he murmured softly, "When a rabbit kicks the ground with his hind legs what's he doing?"

"That's called stamping," Mr. Nomura answered back in a small, yet clearly audible voice. "The rabbit is a very cautious animal. What's more, he's also faint-hearted and so high strung that he gets easily stressed out, and, whenever he gets anxious and agitated, he starts kicking the ground fiercely with his hind legs."

Together with his onigiri rice ball, Riku swallowed a cry of surprise. So all that kicking, he realized, was Jones getting agitated!

"The rabbit also stamps," Mr. Nomura continued, "to warn his friends of any looming danger, such as whenever he sees a predator approaching. The rabbit doesn't have a voice, so he sends signals instead through actions like that, you see."

"Wait, what? The rabbit doesn't have a voice?"

"It's dangerous for a prey, such as a rabbit, to cry out. In general plant-eating animals—the so called grazers or herbivories—which get eaten by meat-eating animals— the so called carnivores—tend not to cry out that much."

Animals that get eaten don't cry out! Riku thought, his hair standing on end at the revelation.

Thick clouds brewed unnoticed and quickly blocked the sunlight. The weather suddenly turned chilly.

"That marten we saw a little while ago was tiny, but it's still a carnivore. The sound it makes when it threatens to attack is like the sound a rattlesnake makes, so you can imagine, it's really terrifying."

"Do martens eat rabbits?"

"Yeah, they're the natural enemies of rabbits."

Riku couldn't forget that graceful and powerful jump of the meat-eating marten. How majestic and beautiful it was! Then, in the next moment, Riku felt sad that the rabbit, the marten's prey, was voiceless.

"Although they're mute, rabbits have big ears for detecting the presence of enemies. And furthermore they're terrific breeders, giving birth to lots and lots of offspring. So even if they get eaten their population doesn't dwindle."

I get it! Rabbits live under the constant threat of being eaten, and that's why they don't play... I see that clearly now.

"So then, are rabbits born to get eaten?"

"Not only rabbits. All living things on Earth give their lives. That's the way God made this place."

Unawares, the following words came flying out of Riku's mouth: "What about humans?" A large clump of snow fell from a tree with a thud.

"A living thing inevitably dies, right? But it can't decide how it's going to die. The same goes for humans."

Riku wanted to say something more but his mind went blank, the topic too difficult to grasp.

"Want some chocolate?"

Mr. Nomura gave him a chocolate bar. The sweetness melting away on Riku's tongue gave his body warm relief.

"When your body temperature falls, you get more exhausted than you think you might, so sweet stuff tastes even better. It's great, right?"

"Yes."

Mr. Nomura looked up at the sky, and said, "Let's go home soon. Mountain weather is volatile, it changes easily. Seems like a storm's brewing."

When Mr. Nomura stood up, Riku said with resolution, "Mr. Nomura!"

"Yes?"

"I want to know more about mountains and animals and stuff. Please teach me."

Mr. Nomura laughed, as if to be embarrassed, and then said, "Sure thing!"

They went down the mountain, drenching with sweat as they walked. All along the way, though, in Riku's mind's eye, that golden marten kept jumping all the time.

Here Comes Uncle Bear

"I hear you've got children from Fukushima over?"

At dinner time there appeared an uncle with a bright red face and glaring eyes.

Etched on his forehead were three deep lines of wrinkles, and, from his nose to mouth, a clear line ran down, making his face resemble, Riku thought, a red ogre.

This uncle announced out loud, "I've brought some venison sashimi," and stepped inside rudely, as if the house belonged to him, and, taking long strides, went on to disappear into the kitchen.

"That person's a hunter," Mr. Nomura said, adding, "or rather he used to be in the old days."

Which means he's not a hunter at present, Riku guessed. Named Gen-san, this uncle was deep-voiced with a short neck, and his hair was stiff and thick and mixed with white hair. His arms were overgrown with shaggy hair, and his hands were so thick they looked like gloves.

Although he looked like Enma Daioh, the overlord of the underworld, he was very friendly and smiling. Small children, when they see one, can immediately spot a person who's fond of children, so they began monkeying around and grappling with Gen-san in no time at all, causing such a rough-and-tumble racket before the low dining table.

Riku worried over whether he should intervene and say, "Come on now, stop messing around and eat your food." But no matter how you looked at it, Gen-san, the adult, was egging on the kids, who were now either climbing up onto Gen-san's shoulders or twining all around his legs, while Gen-san, with his stubby, log-like arms, was vigorously, yet carefully, throwing them down.

Soon, though, Mrs. Nomura came over with a platter of red meat.

"This is deer meat. Have you ever tried?"

Riku shook his head.

"It's really good. The meat's chilled, but once you put it in your mouth, it's going to melt away."

"Oh no," Chaco said, placing her hands on her cheeks.

"Poor deer," Seyla said in a tearful voice.

Ryo and Masato exchanged looks with each other and went, "Ooh."

Then, all eyes gathered on Riku—What, me? Fearfully sandwiching a morsel between his chopsticks, Riku dabbed it in some soy sauce before popping it into his wide open mouth. Whoa! So cold! The meat inside was melting away. It was crisp and had a strange feel on the tongue, at once soft and sweet, and it didn't smell bad at all.

"...Delicious!"

Gen-san flashed a smile and laughed and, with his chest stuck out, bragged, "That's right, it is delicious!" Then, poking Mr. Nomura's shoulder, he added, "Did you hear that? Says it's delicious." He was like a big kid.

The other children, all at once, began to reach out for the delicacy with their chopsticks. And, soon enough, the word "Delicious" came flying out of their mouths too.

"Gen-san works in the field of bear conservation. He nicely sends back to the mountains any bear who strays into the village. You should see what he does, he attacks the bear with his bare hands. It's amazing!"

Gen-san was joyfully pouring some beer into his glass.

When Riku asked, "Do you eat bears, too?" Gen-san gulped down the beer and sighed before saying, "In the past, yes, but not anymore. There's plenty to eat these days, after all."

That evening, at the fireplace, the children all sat around Gen-san and listened to him tell stories about bears.

In the huge hearth, logs were ablaze with dancing red flames, making everyone's face glow with the light of the fire swaying to and fro. The bonfire-like smell of the house now began to seep into the fabric of each and everyone's clothes. Mr. Nomura sat some distance away, cross-legged. Riku and the other children were watching the fire burn, leaning so forward into the dancing flames that they seemed to be in danger of falling into the hearth.

Gen-san, while gesturing with his hands and body, talked about a contest of wits between bears and humans. The story was a bit cruel, but exciting nonetheless.

"The bear, you see, is the king of the forest, and he

possesses a power that no human has. Do you know what that is?"

The children began to shout out whatever came to mind: "Scratching with sharp claws!" "Biting with fangs!"

"That's right, Claws!" Gen-san said. "The claws of a bear are razor-sharp, and his arms are extremely powerful too. If a bear attacks you with his claws, you're mincemeat. Humans just don't stand a chance."

Masato and Chaco cowered in fear as Gen-san gestured wildly at them like a bear swinging his claws.

Riku, though, was impressed, finding Gen-san's gesture very true to life. This person, he thought, must always be earnest in whatever he does.

"The bear has a good nose," Gen-san continued. "He's protected by thick fur and layers of fat, can smell a human from far away, and even though he's humongous, he's agile and quick-footed. What's more, he's a great tree climber as well, and, on top of everything, he's got a good head. In the old days, he used to be worshipped as the god of the forest, you know. Now children, can any of you tell me what a bear eats?"

"Animals!" "Humans!" "Honey."

Gen-san roared with laughter—Ho-Ho! Ha-Ha-Ha!

"Bears won't eat a person unless there's a really good reason. In fact, the only time a bear would attack a human being is when it's afraid and agitated. Humans are too greasy—on account of their oily, fatty deposits. In fact, if a bear eats a person he's going to suffer abdominal pain."

That must be true, Riku thought, humans seem like they'd taste awful.

"Bears are omnivores so they'll eat anything. Just like humans. Their favorite food is nuts; even though they sometimes target a beehive or an ant colony, they eat nuts the most. Which is why they live in the forest. In a good forest there's plenty of nuts and other foods to eat. In other words, what we call a good forest is a forest in which we find bears living, get it? The fact that bears live in a certain forest is proof that that particular forest is a rich and plentiful one, a forest where there's enough of all kinds of foods for bears to survive on."

Seyla asked, "What kind of a forest does a bear like?"

"The bear likes a bright forest. Why, I'm sure you guys also like bright places better than dark places, don't you? The same goes for bears too. Living things can't inhabit a dark forest where no light shines through. And when living things stop living in a forest, the forest turns into something like a vacant house. Do you understand? Unless there are living things living there, a forest dies. And do you know what happens when a forest dies? Even the sea dies. Why? Because the forest and sea are connected. The sea may seem to be so very far away from the forest, but it is, in fact, connected by the river. The rich nutrients of the forest, flowing through the river, pour into the ocean. As a result, the sea becomes abundant, allowing many living things to live. So if we have an abundant forest and an abundant sea, we humans, you see, can keep our belly's full without having to toil.

Gen-san stared into the face of every child, one by one, and asked, "Understand?" Riku and everybody else just sat there, stunned.

"I suppose it was a bit too difficult for you all. Well, anyway, life in the forest used to be ideal for bears; that's when they were, at one time, the happiest. But the forest began to get thinner, that is to say, it began to lose its richness, its life-giving power—so much so that the food supply for the bears have diminished. And that's why, to survive, they've begun to come down to the village. In the village, there's food, after all. Humans are afraid of the bear, though. But even the bear is afraid of humans. That's because, at the end of the day, the only thing that can defeat a bear is a human being. For the bear, the king of the forest, the greatest enemy is none other than the human being. Which is why, whenever it sees a person, the bear gets excited and, to protect itself, launches an attack. But the bear is a clever animal, so it knows that if it attacks a human it too will get attacked in return, and possibly, killed. So the bear really doesn't want to have anything to do, as much as possible, with humans. But the young, inexperienced bear finding it terribly tough to survive on his own, ends up coming down to the village."

"Don't bears live with their family?" Masato asks.

"Sure, the mother bear is in charge of child rearing, and the bear, during his early years as a cub, spends his time together with his brothers and sisters and his mother, but once he grows up, he must become independent and look for his own feeding ground. The young bear has to live as distant as possible from where he was born. In the world of the bear, that is the law. In a good forest, though, there's always an older bear who's already staked out that forest as his own territory—his own turf. So, unless the young bear finds his own forest, he'll starve to death. Every now and again, such a young bear, hungry and desperately out of options, comes down to the village.

"Every one of them is just skin-and-bones. If left to wander around the village, such a bear might end up attacking a person, so the normal thing to do is to shoot it dead. But I don't want to kill any bear, so I do my best to persuade the bear to calm down and drive him away back to the mountains; but without any food, the only thing left for him to do is starve to death."

Gen-san said those last words with such glaring eyes that Riku as well as the other children all fell silent and became sad.

"Poor bear," Chaco said, her eyes filled with tears.

Seyla, on the other hand, was outraged, asking, "Why did the bear's food disappear from the forest?"

"We've got to deliver food to the bears in the forest!" declared Ryo.

Riku, with his lips sealed in a straight line, kept silent.

"Human beings, after all, have forgotten how vitally important the forest really is. But ancient humans knew. Our ancestors of that time may not have had knowledge, but they had wisdom—an intelligence for survival. They knew, deep inside their hearts, what was really important. Sadly, though, people gradually forgot this wisdom and began to fill their heads with just facts and figures. Then, one day, the guy with nothing but all that kind of knowledge—with nothing but that kind of junk info— came to throw his weight around and have his own way. And that's why the world's become so messed up. The nuclear power station is a great example of what I mean; anything that's made from just knowledge inevitably ends up going out of control and wreaking havoc."

"Gen-san," Mr. Nomura said, locking eyes with him. The children took a deep breath, acutely sensing a prickly mood in the air. Such a thing frequently happened in Minamisōma too. When grownups began to argue things got complicated.

Gen-san sighed with a shrug and threw a log into the fire.

"You know, when it comes to firewood, you can't just use any old log from any old tree. Some trees pop, you see, and if you use the logs of such trees, they're going to pop and make sparks fly and end up burning down the house."

Riku wondered, Are humans so evil? Are humans bad for the earth? "How are humans different from animals?"

Gen-san laughed and said to Riku, "What a demanding question you ask! Humans have what's called self-awareness. That's what's most different. Humans think, using words. Animals, on the other hand, only act on their instincts. Sure, they make decisions too, but they don't dilly-dally, going should I stay or should I go, you know. In the first place they don't know any words, so they can't think, at least not in the thoughtful, self-examining way we do. There's a saying that goes 'Man is a thinking reed.' Do you understand what that means? Man thinks, and that's why man worries. Animals don't worry, and that's why they're carefree."

Why was it that humans, unlike other animals, pondered and worried over things?

If animals were free of worry, wasn't it far better, then, to be animals?

Why was I born human?

While Riku's mind was reeling with such deep thoughts, he suddenly felt far removed from everyone else seated around the fireplace, as if he, alone, had floated up in the air and was hovering above them.

That night, Masato became homesick and began to cry.

Was it because he was no longer stressed? Or was it because he had been so deeply moved by Gen-san's story? It was probably both. Sitting near Masato, who was slowly sobbing convulsively under his futon cover, Riku quietly rubbed his back.

"Mommy, Mommy!" Masato was crying, his face a crimson red as he sucked his thumb while shedding huge drops of tears; he had completely gone back to being a baby.

"It's all right, Masato. We're all here together with you…"

After having said so, Riku felt strangely embarrassed, as if he had become Masato's mother. Riku, too, used to have his own back rubbed in the same way by his mother. His mother, Riku remembered, used to even sing to him in a soft voice, Hushabye, Hushabye!

Riku didn't have a mother anymore.

Whenever grownups found this out, they would suddenly look sad and knit their brows to show how sorry they were for him. Riku, though, had never felt sorry for himself, so he always ended up feeling uncomfortable.

Riku's mother passed away when Riku was in the third grade, which was two years ago.

But time in Riku's mind was so twisted and warped he couldn't tell if this was a long time ago or if it was recent.

At that time Riku had cried a lot. It was so sad. But this sadness didn't last.

To Riku today, those days now seem to be mostly made up of silent, wordless moments of just looking up at the sky from somewhere on a mountain of pure white snow, of moments lost in extreme quiet, in serene silence, in being alone. This being alone, this solitude, wasn't a sad feeling, though, nor was it lonely and alienating; it was just a feeling that you got when everything fell silent, when your emotions felt frozen.

Some time back Aunt Midori had surprised Riku when she told him, "You stopped laughing so we got very worried."

Riku doesn't know what happens after a person dies. All he knows is that, once a person dies, he will never be able to meet that person again—Mother's body was cremated, so there's no hope.

But even though in his head he clearly understood this, he couldn't help feeling that she was still around somewhere, that she still existed, though they couldn't get together again. Riku couldn't help feeling this way. There are many things, he reasoned, a child cannot do on his own, and, since I'm still a child, that must be why I can't meet Mother yet, surely. So when I become an adult, I just might be able to go look for her.

Riku, in his daydreams, was waiting for the day when he'd set out on a journey to find his mother.

But now Riku was beginning to feel that, while taking care of small children, he himself could never go back to being a baby like Masato.

He was never going to see his mother anymore.

Mother had died.

When Riku's mother got sick, nobody ever imagined that she was going to die, not at such a young age. Of course, she was going to regain her health, or so everyone naturally thought.

It's all right. She'll get better soon, just wait and see, everyone would say and laugh. Even Aunt Midori had said so, even Yuta's mom had said so.

But in truth Riku's mother's condition was very poor. It was so poor, in fact, that the doctor had no choice but to give up the treatment. To this day, Riku remained unsure of the name of the illness. He had asked several times, but had forgotten nonetheless. All Riku understood was that his mother was gradually getting thinner and smaller.

After she was admitted into the hospital, Riku and his father went to see her there every day.

Life alone with his father was lonesome but fresh and interesting. Father messed up a lot, though: he'd end up burning toast until it was a crisp, deep black; he'd forget to air the laundry and leave all the clothes wrinkled up... The two of them would visit Riku's mother in the hospital to report such incidents and roar with laughter together, free of any worries. Because Mother was surely going to get well again.

A little while later she was discharged and came to live in the house. A home-visit nurse and Aunt Midori took care of Mother then. Mother was better now, Riku had thought; even though she was still unable to eat her meals and was bedridden, Riku believed that she would get well again.

"I'm sorry, Riku," her mother would say, but Riku didn't like to hear her apologize. His mother hadn't done anything wrong, so it was strange that she was apologizing. When she apologized to him like that, her words would suddenly send shivers down his spine and make him feel cold inside. And that's why Riku would get a little gloomy and cast his eyes down.

At a nearby shrine, Riku joined his hands together and prayed for his mother, saying, "May Mommy get well." This place was where Riku and his mother would often enjoy a stroll together, where Riku would catch a lot of beetles found on the zelkova trees standing in the precincts of the shrine. Every time they came here, Mother would always pray to God, saying, "May Riku grow up to be healthy and strong."

And that's why Riku also prayed.

Then one day in autumn, when the sycamore trees in the school playground had already turned brown, it happened. Aunt Midori showed up to pick Riku up while he was still in class. The two of them, instead of going home, went to the hospital. It was the same hospital where Riku's mother had been admitted before, so Riku thought that his mother had become ill and hospitalized again.

When they went into her ward, she was lying in bed. Seated beside her was Father, holding Mother's hand. Then Riku, with his father's arm wrapped around him, looked into his mother's face. He couldn't tell if her eyes were seeing him. She wasn't saying anything anymore. Riku kept his gaze on his mother's face anyway, when he noticed that her eyes were gradually turning white.

At that moment Riku felt as though he had been sucked into his mother's eyes. The surroundings of the room—every single thing inside it—had dissolved into her milky eyes, where a world of pure-white, a world where all color was absent, just as it was in the white kingdom, was spread out before him in every direction.

Mommy.

Riku's nose suddenly stung as tears began to spill over.

Masato was already breathing peacefully, so Riku quietly left him and crawled into his own futon.

Mommy, Mommy… the little child in Riku called out.

This little child still believed that he would one day come face to face with her again. While looking hard into his heart, Riku saw how very sweet, and how very sad, this little child was that he couldn't help but spill more tears.

Hey there, little Riku, the bigger Riku thought. You did really well. You did your best, you hung in there. Well done, Riku.

The Mysterious Boy and the Tonchi

The view was so dazzling Riku had to squint.

Snow crystals—reflecting the sun's rays—were shining iridescently, and the surface of the snowscape was sparkling and shimmering like diamonds.

Wow! What a beautiful day! The sky's like blue cellophane.

A sliver of the sky was showing through the canopy of frost-covered trees hung with icicles and leaves of ice, when suddenly out of nowhere a snowball flew and hit Riku in the face.

"Ow!"

Involuntarily seizing his face, Riku was surprised and shouted, "Who's there?"

From the depths of the forest came the bright, cackling sounds of laughter, the dappled sunlight quaking along. Riku, slowly but surely, opened his eyes wide, when a shadow glided through the groves.

Gotcha! Riku thought.

With firm resolve, Riku, too, shaped a snowball and flung it into the air, but it struck a tree trunk and burst into smithereens.

"Ha, ha! You're a lousy shot!" a voice said out of nowhere and everywhere, ricocheting off of the many trees of the forest, alarming the birds so much that they shrieked and flew away. Riku couldn't tell at all where the voice was coming from.

Ha ha! Ha ha! Ha ha! You suck!

Snowballs were whizzing through the air, one after the other.

"Whoa!"

Hiding behind a large tree, Riku made lots of snow balls and arranged them at his feet in preparation for battle.

When he peeped out to monitor the situation, yet another snowball flew his way.

Did that one come from the right? Riku frantically threw a snowball back in that direction.

A boy in a light blue parka ran through the trees. This time, though, Riku clearly saw his figure; he was looking straight at Riku, and, in a mocking gesture, pulling one eyelid down while sticking out his tongue.

Damn!

Riku chased after the boy through the multitude of trees which, with their branches raised high in the air, appeared to be dancing, and amid all this dancing, the boy was taking huge strides and bounding right through them, gently whirling up clouds of snow dust that were as beautiful as dusts of gold. Riku stopped to admire these snow crystals glittering beautifully in the air, but the boy turned around to look at Riku and, once again, pulled one eyelid down and stuck out his tongue.

Oh, come on! Riku thought as he was about to resume his chase, when he stopped in his tracks, stunned.

Behind the boy was one more child.

No, wait, not a child.

It was small, standing just around twenty centimeters tall, and it had a thick, bushy cluster of silver hair. A white monkey? No, a child Yeti? No way! A hairy elf?

Riku rubbed his eyes many times and tried to make sure. It was a creature he had never seen before; with pointy ears standing straight up and eyes taking up half its face, it even looked like a horned owl. Its jet-black almond-shaped eyes had no room for any eye white, its nose was as pink as a rabbit's and connected to a very big mouth that was wearing a delightful grin, and its head was huge, and its body monkey-like—just what on earth was this thing…?

Chasing the two of them deeper and deeper into the forest, Riku began to pant and came to a stop.

The boy was waiting for him.

Riding on top of the boy's shoulder was that strange creature.

When Riku approached and took a good look, it hid bashfully behind the boy's head. His large eyes were like two black glass beads, and his long eyelashes were shining with snow crystals.

"Says he gets shy, being stared at so much like that," the boy said, looking at Riku's face and smirking. The dark-eyed elf nodded, uh-huh.

The boy's skin was very white and, with the light blue of the parka casting a glow on his face, he looked like an ice sculpture.

When Riku asked, "Is that… an animal…?" the boy answered, "He's a tonchi."

"What's that?"

"A tonchi's a tonchi."

Can't argue with that, Riku thought.

"Hey, let's play some more. What game should we play next?"

Riku became suddenly scared.

Where am I?

Riku was starting to feel that if he went on playing he might never be able get back home.

"I should be heading back now. Everyone'll get worried. Where do you live, by the way?"

The boy fell silent and suddenly said in a low voice, "Right here. This is my home."

"Huh? You mean this forest?"

The boy looked at the tonchi and nodded deeply.

When Riku laughed and said, "No child can live in a forest like this all by himself, that's impossible!" the boy seemed slightly offended, his face turning a little sour. Then, his hair, even though there wasn't any wind blowing, gently stood on end. No sooner had Riku thought, hey, than his body was propelled into the air until he landed on the bed of snow, rear end first.

The boy hadn't done anything; he hadn't lifted a finger. The only thing that had happened was that Riku had fallen; a wind had blown, and Riku had been blown away by the blast of this wind. That was all that had happened, surely.

"What the hell? I just played with you to give you some company, you know, seeing that you were feeling so lonely."

Surprised by such talk from the boy, Riku yelled back, "I'm not lonely!"

As Riku watched him from the ground, he saw several rays of dappled sunlight streaming past from behind the boy's back like so many pillars of light, turning him into a great black shadow as he approached Riku.

"Liar! You were all weepy and crying."

The tonchi jumped off from the boy's shoulder and landed on the ground. Then, in a move that was as swift as a marten's, he leaped onto Riku's chest, where Riku felt the creature's weight down to the bone. The tonchi's hands and feet were hairless, his skin bare, his fingers very small, and he was all pink and soft like a hamster. The tonchi planted his face on Riku's nose and stared at him.

"Hey...What are you doing?"

In the tonchi's large, dark eyes Riku saw the reflection of his own face staring back. This face was the face of Riku when he was younger; it was the face of Riku two years ago.

Suddenly conscious of how lonely he was, Riku, with empty courage, snapped back, "I'M NOT LONELY!"

His eyes opened.

A dream?

Feeling numb all over, Riku couldn't move at all. Around his chest area, the lingering heaviness of the creature was still vivid and fresh. As Riku remained motionless, he stared at the ceiling, only to see the fair face of the boy appear and descend.

Then, at that moment, as his head reeled and his heart beat heavily, going thumpity-thump, Riku remembered.

It's him!

Riku jumped to his feet and put on his socks.

It's him! I know it's him! I'm sure of it!

Wearing a jacket over his jersey, Riku walked on tiptoe, so as not to wake up the other children, and opened the sliding paper-door.

It's him! It's him!

He hurried down the corridor all by himself, braving the eyes of the stuffed hawk glaring his way, before he stood in front of Yoichi's room, blowing out white breath. The light from inside was leaking through the sliding paper-door.

"Yoichi-san, are you awake?"

Moments later, Yoichi's voice was heard from inside.

"Yes, I'm awake. You're up very early, aren't you? What's the matter?"

The door slid open and Yoichi appeared, clad in his usual king-sized sleeveless jacket, the *chanchanko*, looking a little sleepy. "I was nodding off, actually."

To Yoichi-san, who was now scratching his head while taking a big yawn, Riku asked frantically, "That boy, that boy in the photograph?"

"What? What boy in the photograph?"

Oh, no. I can't explain in words.

"Please come with me," Riku said, leading Yoichi by the hand before he knew it, toward that dark room too terrifying to enter alone.

When Riku quietly slid the door open, a pillar made a creaking sound. The room was cold as an ice cave. Neatly lined around a great shining black Buddhist altar were the photographs of the faces, faces, and faces of the past.

When Riku said, "This boy," pointing to the brand-new looking photograph found at the end of the row, Yoichi absentmindedly opened his mouth and flicked his eyes from the photograph to Riku and back again.

"That's my little brother."

Their breath vapors fused in a fuzzy haze of white.

"Little brother?"

"That's right. But he died several years ago."

At that moment Yoichi's face looked different than it usually did; his eyes, his nostrils, and even his mouth appeared like holes drilled open by a woodpecker.

"So, what about Taiju? Is there anything wrong?"

"Taiju?"

"Yeah, that's his name. Why are you talking about my little brother?"

Unsure of how to answer, Riku fell silent. Yoichi let out a sigh and looked up at the photograph. His sigh sounded very much like the one Riku's father occasionally let out—a sad sound, like a current of cool air leaking through the crack of a door or window.

"My younger brother was born with a heart condition. He couldn't go outside and play, since he'd have a seizure quickly if he did. I used to feel so sorry for him."

"I met this boy."

"Who? Taiju?"

Riku nodded, before adding, "In my dream..."

The moment he said this Riku suddenly grew uneasy.

Yoichi was staring, motionless, at the photograph of the boy.

"What was Taiju doing?"

Riku, feeling relieved, relaxed his shoulders.

"He was playing with that strange creature you talked about, the tonchi," Riku said, nodding with a serious look on his face as Yoichi blinked in surprise.

"Is that right? So he was together with the tonchi. What was the tonchi like?"

"He was small, quick, and had these gigantic eyes that were all iris and completely black, and his nose was pink like a rabbit's, and he looked like a horned owl and a space alien and a Yeti and a monkey and a human—a really kooky creature."

Riku's nostrils were flaring as he spoke, so Yoichi couldn't help but burst out into laughter.

"So that's what he looked like! Was Taiju playing with the tonchi?"

"The two of them were getting along really well."

"I see. That's very good, I'm glad..." Yoichi said, gazing intently at Riku's face, before adding, "Thank you for telling me. I really mean that."

Riku felt somewhat like he was going to lose all his

strength and sink down to the floor in exhaustion.

He believed me. Good.

But what was up with that dream anyway?

Yoichi lit a candle before the altar and, sitting up straight on the floor with his legs folded underneath, lit a stick of incense. Riku, too, sat down next to Yoichi, and then the two of them quietly joined their hands in prayer.

When Yoichi rang the altar bell—ding—Riku remembered his mother.

Won't Mommy appear in my dreams too?

I don't care if it's a dream; as long as she comes to see me.

"Why do you think Taiju came to you, Riku?" Yoichi said, looking at Riku in wonder.

"He said that I was feeling lonely, so he felt sorry and decided to play with me, to give me company." Riku tried to speak normally as possible, without changing his expression. "My mother passed away two years ago, so that's why… surely…"

Yoichi silently laid his right hand over Riku's left hand and gave it a tight squeeze.

He then simply said under his breath, "I wish Taiju would appear in my dreams too. I'd like that."

Riku, too, in his own gentle way, squeezed Yoichi's hand in return.

On the morning of the fourth day, around the time when everyone finished eating breakfast, the staff arrived riding in a big station wagon.

"Hey, how's it going everybody? Have you all been doing well?"

Riku had been away from them just for three days now, but he realized how much he had been missing all of them.

The children welcoming their older brothers and sisters were all going crazy with excitement.

The staff members, though, took a look at Riku and became surprised, saying something along the lines of, "Hey, you look somewhat different! You look a little more like a grownup, you know."

"What! It's just been three days!"

Mr. Nomura was all smiles as he gazed at Riku, his eyes gentle, yet glaring and distant.

In the morning they all went snow sledding.

They slid downhill until they got dog-tired, and with their underwear all soggy with sweat, they had to change their clothes before lunchtime. So Riku, Ryo, and Masato all took a souvenir photo of themselves, buck naked. The firewood stove, as it burned, with the children's underwear hung around it, was clanging and breathing out clouds of white steam, turning the room so hot that Riku and the other kids were growing sweaty.

"It's like summer," Ryo complained. "We came all the way to Hokkaido, and for what? With this heat, this might as well be tropical Okinawa."

"All right boys and girls! Starting in the afternoon, we're going to be making some really, really cold ice cream!"

These staff members, who turned anything into fun and games, were awesome, declaring to make ice cream with snow.

"You put some milk and sugar and fresh cream in a plastic bottle, close the cap, and roll the bottle around in salted snow. Okay then, let's start filling up this plastic bag with snow."

Seyla and Chaco got to work, shoveling snow into the bag.

"Dig the middle and make a hole in the snow!"

Masato roughly scraped out the snow in the bag with both hands like a dog, so everyone got smeared with snow.

"You're overdoing it!" Ryo said while putting in two cups worth of salt into the hollowed out hole.

"Okay, let's now put the plastic bottle inside!"

The plastic bottle containing ice cream ingredients was placed inside the hole in the bag, which was then tied up tightly. This bag was then placed inside an even thicker plastic bag and was to be wound around with gummed tape and shaped into a ball. The duty of winding the tape was assigned to Riku.

"Be sure you wind the tape properly. If you don't, the bag's going to tear open."

All that was left to be done now was for everyone to roll the ball around so that the ingredients inside would get mixed well. It didn't matter if they threw it around or kicked it around; they just had to keep rolling it around like mad.

"Roll that thing away with all you've got, if you want to eat great-tasting, super yummy ice cream!"

"Yeah!"

Ryo's kick, without fail, sent the ball vigorously flying

into the air, as everyone watched, with their mouths wide open, the taped up ball rolling down the gently inclined slope of a roadway where the snow had been cleared away.

"It's dangerous, so I'll go," Riku said and ran after the ball. The snow, though, was hard and slippery, making it difficult to run. That Ryo, he's always overdoing things.

When Riku finally caught up with the ball and stooped to pick it up, something jumped onto it.

"Whoa, what?"

Surprised, Riku, once again, fell spectacularly, rear end first.

What the hell?

On top of the ball was the tonchi, grinning with his almond-shaped jet-black eyes and his nose-linked mouth.

Riku rubbed his eyes again and again, his rear end still on the ground.

Is this a dream too?

The tonchi, while twitching and twisting his long hands and feet, with his large head cocked to one side, was looking at Riku.

Really?

The tonchi began to roll the ball.

"No, no! Don't!!"

Just like an acrobatic dancer in a circus, the tonchi was balancing himself on the ball, his long arms raised while striking a pose. Riku rubbed his eyes over and over again; but it wasn't a dream.

That tonchi was now doing a handstand on the ice cream ball. There was no doubt about it. There was a strange creature there, looking like a horned owl, a space alien, a

Yeti, an unidentifiable, unknown, mysterious entity.

"Hey there, Tonchi, you're real, after all!"

The tonchi, with a happy look on his face, kept flipping, again and again, into a handstand on the ball, reminding Riku of a space alien dressed in a fur coat. "Ha, ha, ha!"

Finally, though, the tonchi fell off the ball, having gotten carried away, and was now rolling his eyes and staggering to his feet, feeling dizzy. He looked like a drunk, or a sleep-deprived horned owl.

"Okay, you can return the ball to me now. We're going to make some ice cream."

Hearing Riku say so, the tonchi stuck his tiny forefinger into his mouth and shook his head, disappointed.

From above, one of the staff members—an older brother—was now anxiously calling out to Riku.

"Are you all right? Need any help?"

Riku shouted back in a hurry, "I'm all right!"

"Look, everyone's going to see you."

The tonchi, blinking his eyes, seemed sad.

"Sorry, Tonchi."

Riku lifted the ball, waved in the older brother's direction, and then turned around to look at the tonchi again. He was trying to follow Riku back, so Riku said to him, "It's all right. I've got friends. Why don't you go back and stay by Taiju's side; give him company instead."

The tonchi nodded, uh-huh, and, tilting his head, flashed a smile before hopping and loping away until he disappeared into the snow.

Riku, feeling relieved while also feeling as if he had just awakened from a dream, took a deep breath before running back toward everybody.

He's real, he's real…

He's R-E-A-L! REAL! Wow!

Riku kicked the ice ball with all his might.

Okay, it's finally time to tear off the tape around the ball and take out the plastic bottle from the bag.

"It's hardened!"

The children broke into cheers, and, sitting on the snow, began to share the freshly made ice cream and eat to their heart's content.

"So cold!"

"Yummy!"

When Riku was playing, and even when he was eating the ice cream together with everyone, Riku couldn't help but feel as if somebody was quietly watching him from far away.

Taiju must be longing to play with all of us here, Riku thought restlessly, as he kept thinking that that boy in the light blue parka might be standing somewhere, hiding behind a grove.

It probably was the first time so many children had visited his home, so that's why Taiju, feeling thrilled, might have appeared. He surely must have wanted to play.

Putting the ice cream into a plastic cup, Riku dug a hole under a tree quietly, so as not to be seen by anybody, and placed the cup in there. Just like his father always served a cup of coffee for his absent mother, Riku wanted to offer and share his ice cream with Taiju.

I'm sorry about yesterday. The next time you appear

for me in my dreams I promise I'll play like there's no tomorrow, okay?

Then, from inside the snow, the tonchi poked his face out. After brushing off the snow on his fur, he heaved up the cup of ice cream with his tiny hands and held it in his arms before taking a few light jumps and hopping away. By the time Riku snapped out of his bewilderment, the tonchi had already vanished. Everything had happened in the blink of an eye.

"Tonchi, be sure to deliver that ice cream to Taiju, you hear?"

As he was about to head back toward everybody, Riku noticed that Mr. Nomura, who had been chopping firewood at a slightly removed distance, was gazing in the direction the tonchi had gone.

He had the same look in his eyes as when he'd found the wild marten in the mountain.

Suddenly Riku remembered Yoichi's words: "…my father said he'd seen the tonchi."

Mr. Nomura's eyes were shimmering gold.

The Night of the Northern Lights

The last night of the five-day, four-night homestay saw everyone—from the mothers of the neighborhood and Mrs. Nomura to the staff and children—making preparations for a farewell party.

"Tonight, we're going to have a fabulous *Jingisukan* party! *Jingisukan*, which is named after Genghis Khan, is a Hokkaido specialty, you know!"

Riku chopped a lot of cabbage. He had become an expert cook, since he'd been helping his father in the kitchen ever since his mother had passed on.

"That's amazing, Riku, such masterful knife handling!" Mrs. Nomura said, pleasing Riku so much he put on the air of a head chef.

Mrs. Nomura lit an old-fashioned *kamado* furnace which she said she didn't normally use, adding, "I'd really like all of you to try the rice that's cooked with this furnace."

She stooped down and, while spilling tears like rain, blew into a bamboo blower to kindle a fire.

The children, seeing the *kamado* furnace for the first time, were delighted and stoked. Once the fire started, rice was washed in a large, iron pot, which was then heaved onto the furnace.

"Okay, we've got to keep the lid on now, until the rice is fully cooked. There's no removing it halfway through, even if a hungry baby starts crying."

Riku saw, at that moment, that Mrs. Nomura, who was always very energetic and loud, was actually remembering Taiju probably whenever she saw Riku and the other kids.

In turn, Riku realized how fond of Mrs. Nomura he was when he heard her say, with her eyes narrowed, "The rice is going to get cooked so deliciously your cheeks are going to fall off!"

Arranged neatly on the table now was a row of griddles for the culinary delight that was to follow: the Mongolian mutton barbecue known as the *Jingisukan-nabe*.

"What's this? What a strange shape!" mischievous Masato said, putting on a griddle over his head. Into these iron, helmet-like dome-shaped pans, everyone began to toss in mutton, bean sprouts and cabbage before making them all sizzle in there, and shortly after, when everyone got a sniff of the aroma that began to waft in the air—a fusion of sweet sauce mixed with the meat broth—tummies began to rumble. Riku and all his friends, with their first Mongolian mutton barbecue spread out before them, were having the time of their life.

Gen-san, once again, came to see the kids with plenty of fresh venison. He began to laugh after asking the older brothers and sisters whether they thought the venison was good or not; thanks to his super imposing voice, though, they were sort of half-coerced into saying that they found the meat delicious. Yoichi, too, joined everyone surrounding the Mongolian mutton barbecue. Riku couldn't believe that he was going to soon part from all these wonderful people.

Only four days had passed, yet, to Riku, everybody here felt like family now. He was so happy, in fact, that he wanted to scream out, from the top of his lungs, I love you, everyone! I love you!

The greater the laughter became at the party, the sadder Riku became, his heart sinking as he fell silent.

In Riku's mind's eye, the memory of that remarkable day of departure came back to life, when the new school term had just begun, and he had disappeared from his classroom. The school building, seen from the gateway that day, appeared very distant. Still, here he was today laughing in the warm, cozy company of so many beautiful people. He never imagined, back then, that such a future as this had been awaiting him.

Riku sat next to Gen-san and fixed his gaze on his profile.

Gen-san felt warm, Riku realized, sitting by his side. It was as if he was a human heater; he was so warm and comforting that Riku felt that if there was anybody to whom he could safely ask about that thing on his mind, that person would be Gen-san.

Riku quietly whispered into his ear, "Gen-san, can I ask you a question?"

Gen-san replied, "Huh?" and, grabbing Riku's neck, drew him to his chest with a jerk. "That depends on what the question's about, boy!"

Gen-san's body smelled of an animal. It was the good old smell Riku had once sniffed when he'd lifted Jones the rabbit—a smell that smelled of dirt and of sweat. Riku whispered, while being subjected now to Gen-san's full nelson headlock, "Have you ever seen an elf, Gen-san?"

"An elf?"

"He stands around twenty centimeters tall, and is furry, and has long hands and feet, and has ginormous eyes, and looks like a horned owl, and has this strange-looking face like a space alien's, and moves quickly and lightly, and prances around in the snow."

"That there's the... tonchi."

I knew it! He knows!

"That fellow's been around in this area since the old days. From a long, long, time ago. So you saw the tonchi?"

Riku nodded hugely. Gen-san, motionless and straight-faced, looked at Riku and gulped down his beer, a drop trickling down from his lips. Then, shaping his eyebrows into an upside down V, he sniffed.

"The tonchi rarely appears in the presence of humans. The tonchi, after all, is the incarnation of the mountain god. But the only time he appears is when..."

"When?"

"When he's about to help a human being. The fact that you saw the tonchi means that something's going on. But the reason cannot be known. God moves in mysterious ways, after all. What God does is unfathomable to humans, do you understand?"

"Do you believe in God, Gen-san?"

"Of course I do."

"Why?"

Folding his muscular, hunky arms, Gen-san spoke with authority, "We humans are so proud, aren't we, telling ourselves that we're the lord of creation? If God didn't exist, this world would be at the beck and call of us high and mighty human beings; we'd be running amok, controlling the world as we pleased."

Riku wasn't convinced.

"I don't believe in god, but I still saw the tonchi. Why is that?"

"What's the use of wondering like that? The forest is filled with a great deal of things, a whopping number of animals too. But you rarely get a chance to see them. Why did you get to see the tonchi, you ask? Phooey! Nobody knows such a thing. But you know what? Whether you're talking about a deer, a bear, an elf, or even a ghost, when the time comes, you will meet whatever or whoever it is that you will meet."

"Then, what should you do when you meet it?"

"You be polite, that's what. You can't go wrong with whatever you bump into, if you extend your courtesy. Catch my drift?"

"Thank you, Gen-san," Riku said, nodding hugely again.

Pretending to leave for the restroom, Riku quietly stepped outside the mansion, borrowing Yoichi's tall boots found on the dirt floor in the doorway. The boots were so large they fit loosely, but they hid Riku's legs all the way up to his knees, so it was just right.

Although it was already nighttime it was still faintly light outside, and the snow—smooth and powdery—had begun to fall again.

The snow had been shoveled away, but there was so much piled up already.

Losing his footing in the powdery layer of ice crystals, Riku stepped forward into the kingdom of white, where the snow was trying to blanket the world, to swallow up every existing color and transform the earth into a dominion of monotone white so pure, so sacred, and so divine.

What is snow, Riku wondered as he quietly grabbed a handful of the icy grains.

The world is so full of wonders, so full of unknowns.

The sky was endlessly giving birth to the snow, as Riku called out, Mother, I've come to Hokkaido all by myself.

Then, from the sky came falling down, gently amid the drifting snowflakes, the tonchi. This guy's such a phantom, Riku thought, appearing anywhere out of nowhere without a warning.

The tonchi landed on Riku's shoulder and flashed a grin, and then pointed ahead.

Riku's heart pounded, skipping a beat.

Standing there, in the night, as if to be weightlessly floating like a wisp of cloud, was Taiju, staring into Riku's face.

The tonchi remained on Riku's shoulder, as Taiju glided toward Riku and handed the cup of ice cream to him. Riku accepted it without saying a word. Taiju laughed.

Relieved, Riku said, "Taiju, thank you for playing with me. And, yes, I was feeling lonely. You were right."

The snow absorbed Riku's voice into its grand silence.

"Without being able to see Mother, I was feeling very lonely."

Taiju laughed, as if to say, I know, and waved his hand without saying a word, before becoming transparent and fading away.

A furious wind blew, roaring through the night.

The snow whirled up from the ground and, morphing into a tornado, wrapped around Riku. The tonchi, sucked upward by the blast of wind, was whirling round and round in the air. Riku stretched out his arms and confronted the storm head-on with his entire being, but he felt so disoriented he couldn't tell up from down, nor whether he was still standing or had fallen down. At the same time, his hands and feet were getting comfortably cold and numb. The snow was clinging onto his body like something alive, like the spirit of a dead person.

"Ahhh!"

The wind continued to whirl round and round, launching Riku sky high. The snow, transformed into streaming sashes of white, was being whooshed into the darkness, when, out of the blue, a gaping hole in the night sky opened up and glittered faintly.

Mother…?

A white light, shimmering and rippling like an aurora,

kept flashing on and off above Riku's head like a searchlight and and, after unveiling Taiju from the secret darkness of the night, wrapped around him, before giving off a golden spark and vanishing.

Riku unconsciously covered his eyes.

In the luminous afterglow the snow was shining with a kaleidoscopic brilliance of colors, like an opal, and, for a while in the area, lightly drifting about Riku like glowing fireflies.

It had all happened in the blink of an eye.

When Riku realized, everything was over.

The wind had died down, the sky was dark, and the sounds of everyone's laughter were faintly heard from inside the mansion, as the smoke from the wood burning stove gave off the warm smell of burnt things.

When Riku took a deep breath, though, the back of his nose stung.

Tears slowly welled up in Riku's eyes, so he wiped them and his runny nose on the sleeve of his parka.

It already seems like a long time ago, Riku thought, when I practiced snowshoeing over this snow, where I kept tumbling down again and again. Everything passes. Even fun things, even painful things. All things pass.

When Riku rubbed his eyes and dusted off the snow on his head and turned around, all fired up with resolve, saying, "Right," he noticed the silhouette of a person in the near distance.

It was Mr. Nomura.

He was standing there, stock-still, looking at Riku. Although it was too dark to see the look on his face, Riku felt Mr. Nomura's eyes burning into him. Then, as Riku just stood there, motionless himself, Mr. Nomura, still in silhouette, stepped cautiously toward Riku, making a crunching sound as he treaded the snow. Then, as if to blanket Riku, the shadow gently enveloped him in a hug.

Mr. Nomura always smells like a bonfire, Riku thought. People sure do come in a variety of smells.

"Thank you," Mr. Nomura said, his hand, swung around Riku's back, brimming with energy.

As Riku wondered why Mr. Nomura was thanking him, the grownup quietly pulled away from the embrace, patted Riku's hair, and laughed, before speaking from his heart.

Never again can you meet someone who has died.

That's a very painful thing, I know. It's like being homesick all the time.

But remember what Gen-san said? When the time comes, you will meet whatever or whoever it is that you will meet.

"Okay, come on now. Let's head back, it's getting cold." Mr. Nomura sniffed and patted Riku's back.

The warm orange glow of a lamp was spilling out from the window as the air rang with happy voices singing.

Following Mr. Nomura's back, Riku advanced, step by step, toward the light, with care and respect.

3

THE TIME OF DEPARTURE

The moment they passed through the ticket gates, voices saying, welcome back, echoed throughout the station building.

The children burst into shouts of joy as Riku shyly waved at the welcoming party—the adults who had come to pick up the kids. An older brother—one of the staff members—held a flag to guide and assemble the children into a small cluster, so as not to stand in the way of pedestrian traffic. The staff had to finish their last roll call and deliver a farewell speech.

The small children, when they saw their mothers, were on the verge of tears, but they resisted the urge and obediently observed the time-honored rules of good group behavior. Masato, with whom Riku was together all the time in Hokkaido, was part of the company of friends that was going to disband at Fukushima Station. He had become completely attached, though, to Riku by now and was clinging to him like a little brother as they walked together. Placing his hand on Masato's shoulder, Riku stretched his back and, lifting his head, took in the view.

I'm back. Back in Fukushima.

Riku felt the eyes of the guardians on him, and when he noticed that his father was there too, his earlobes turned hot.

"Well, Congratulations everyone!" the older brother began. "We've successfully completed the Hokkaido program; there were no accidents, and everyone remains in high spirits. I'm truly pleased. And I'm also very proud of all your efforts. Well done, kids! Let's meet again, and thank you."

All the children shook hands with the older brothers and sisters before embracing each other.

"Masato, take care of yourself, okay?"

Tugging at Riku's held out hand, Masato, while exhaling a warm breath over Riku's earlobe, said, "Guess what? I saw an elf!" Startled, Riku looked squarely into Masato's face; his cheeks were puffed up and his eyes were shining.

"Don't tell anyone, okay? It's a secret."

"Got it…" Riku nodded.

Masato joyfully waved and dashed off. The grownups who'd come to pick him up were a very elderly couple. Huh? Riku thought. Where's his mother?

"Masato's parents died in the tsunami, you know," mumbled a lady staff member who was standing next to Riku. "How bravely everyone's holding on…"

Pointing at Riku, Masato was delightfully shouting out, "That older brother there! He played with me all the time!!"

The grandmother and the grandfather, who was holding Masato in his arms, bowed to Riku many times. Riku, too, removing his hat, politely bowed in return.

Then, Riku ran toward his father who was laughing warmly, with his arms folded.

"I'm home."

"How was it? Did you have fun?" Riku's father said as he tried to carry the rucksack for Riku.

"That's all right. It's not that heavy."

"Is that right?"

"From now on, I'm going to look after myself as much as I can."

Impressed, Riku's father let out a whistle.

"You've manned up, haven't you?"

In Fukushima Station there still were many commuters wearing masks, the expressions on their faces dark, as they rushed here and there throughout the station.

It was different from Hokkaido…

The two of them got into the car parked near the station and headed for Minamisōma.

The rotary before the station plaza was deserted. The restaurants in the station building were open for business, but there were hardly any people around, and in the shopping area shutters stood out.

The atmosphere was heavy in this snowless, grey town.

Here, Riku thought, time seemed to have come to a standstill.

"Hokkaido was fun, right? I bet you didn't even want to come home."

"Umm, I'm happy to be back in Fukushima."

Keeping his hands gripped on the steering wheel, Riku's father looked into Riku's face.

"I see… why?"

"I don't know, but that's how I feel."

"Did you have any trouble getting to the restroom at night?"

"No, well, actually I was a bit afraid because the house was old, but there was an older brother there studying for the entrance exams and he took good care of me."

"I'm glad."

"The snow was amazing! There was even a blizzard when we arrived, howling like crazy. And you know what? I went up the mountain and saw a marten; it was all golden and beautiful."

"Wow! Not even your father has seen a marten, you know." There was a lot Riku wanted to say. But he wasn't sure if he could tell his stories in a way that his father would understand. If I were to tell Dad, a psychiatrist, that I saw a funny-looking elf, what would he say? He'd probably think I was mental.

"There were pictures of you kids uploaded on the Fukushima Kid's blog, so I've been looking at them every day."

Riku nodded and started to say, "You know what?" but then stopped; there was so much to talk about that he became baffled and fell silent.

The late-night hot chocolate, the dream of Taiju, the

dark-eyed tonchi...Should I tell Dad, at this time, about all these things? Will he understand?

No way, impossible!

Riku sighed. The scenery outside looked different—Is this place the same Minamisōma I'd left behind?

Good, good, good, good vibrations—Riku's father was singing breezily, as he usually did while driving.

But Riku understood that it was, once again, mere bravado, that he was just pretending again to appear tough and unconcerned.

Father has become awfully thin, Riku noticed. He must be worn out. Is his work so demanding? The rings under his eyes are dreadful.

Hey Gen-san, look, there's a bear here too, Riku thought amusedly, recalling that the word for rings under the eyes is *kuma*, the same sound as the Japanese character meaning bear.

When they reached home, Riku—perhaps because he felt relieved—curled up under the thick quilt of the *kotatsu* table heater and fell asleep.

Even though he sensed his father draping a blanket over him, he pretended not to know. Riku had returned to his spoiled childhood, for the first time in a long time, and slept tight.

The next morning when Riku woke up, he was in a futon bed, properly dressed in pajamas too, to his surprise.

I was so sound asleep that I didn't even wake up and notice Dad changing my clothes!

The stove was turned on and the room was warm inside. Riku thought, this sure is my home: the six-mat living room, my four-and-a-half-mat bedroom, the two rooms partitioned off by a sliding paper door, and the large kitchen which also doubled as Dad's study.

Getting out of his futon and stepping out of the room, Riku found his father standing in the kitchen cooking, the pleasant aroma of soup stock and soy sauce wafting in the air. Was Dad's back so small? Riku wondered as he gazed vacantly at his father cooking. If Mom were still alive, would he be happier?

"Hey, you're up!" Riku's father said, noticing Riku. Then, with the soup ladle still in his hand, he raised his voice and said, "Happy New Year!"

"Um, happy new year..." Riku rubbed his eyes and looked out the window. It was grey and cloudy.

Oh yeah! That's right. It's New Year's Day today. I totally forgot.

The houses visible from the window, though, still showed no signs of life. The weeds in the yard were withered, since it was winter, and the garden, which hadn't been cared for, was in decay.

Back when Riku used to be in Utsunomiya, every year a children's association would hold a mochi-rice-pounding tournament.

On New Year's Day, Riku would visit the shrine in the neighborhood and, together with his friends he'd meet there, go kite-flying and play video games at home. At night, people from his father's workplace would come over and there'd be a New Year's celebration.

This year was totally different.

Riku washed his face at the sink in the prefab bathroom,

noticing that his face was slightly snow-tanned. Then, realizing he'd left the toothpaste tube open, he thought, oh no, and capped it right away. He also wiped the water drops from the sink bowl; closed the toilet seat lid; neatly arranged the slippers; tidily folded his pajamas, which he'd left lying on the floor in a tangled mess; put away the futon into the closet; tidied up the mess on his desk, and let out a sigh.

Whatever I can do, I must do.

The birthday seat at the table was for Riku's mother.

Placing a bowl of *zoni* soup before her portrait, Riku said, "Enjoy!" Soon, his mother in the photo, Riku felt, was saying thank you back to him. He then joined his hands to offer thanks, saying "*Itadakimasu*," before sipping his *zoni* soup his father had prepared, as white steam rose from the bowl before his mother's image.

It was a quiet meal in the company of his father, who, seated opposite Riku, looked transformed, with his stubbly beard, his dry and disheveled hair, and the boils around his lips. Probably exhausted from working all the time at the hospital, he was speaking less than usual and even cracking lesser jokes—those bad puns—than he normally did to make Riku laugh.

When Riku finished eating his *zoni* soup, his father said, "Here you go, your New Year's gift," and handed him a fancy envelope.

"Thanks, Dad."

Riku put away his New Year's pocket money in a chocolate can kept inside the drawer of his desk, because he was saving as much money as possible. It then occurred to him that, once he had saved up a lot of money, he would one day visit Mr. Nomura's place again.

You can come to play anytime, everyone in that house had told him.

There's no way I'm going to spend this New Year's pocket money now. I'm absolutely going to save it all.

The newspaper and TV were full of nothing but news of nuclear power.

"Both the government and the electric company are really irresponsible," Riku's father grumbled, watching the news. "I'm sure they mean to abandon the citizens of Fukushima…"

The profile of Riku's father, who was facing the TV, appeared nasty and displeased. With the corners of his mouth turned down, he even looked like a stubborn grandfather, Riku thought.

Riku thanked his father for the meal and joined his hands together again, before clearing the table and going to the kitchen, where he stood before the sink and let out a small sigh.

The reading on the dosimeter installed in the veranda was indicating high levels of radiation for today too. Going outside would be prohibited, once again, for many days to come.

On that day, a little past 2 p.m., there was a big aftershock, registering a magnitude of four. The moment the shaking began, the two looked at each other as unpleasant memories came flooding back in their minds. They waited, motionless, for several seconds and, when the quaking settled, Riku's father immediately went online and checked the status of the Fukushima Daiichi Nuclear Power Station. To his and Riku's relief, the early warning system began to relay that there was no need to worry about a tsunami attack.

With nothing else to do, the two of them spent their time lazily watching New Year holiday specials on TV, but it was all so very boring that, soon, Riku's father—after angrily blurting out, "Rubbish!"—tore himself away from the TV, and ended up sitting before his PC. Whether he was working or simply surfing the Net, Riku couldn't tell.

Riku started to play a video game on his gaming console, filling the room with beeping sound effects, but, even though he liked playing alone, he got tired soon.

Keeping his feet under the *kotatsu*, he yawned and stretched and began to sense a hazy unpleasantness spread inside him.

To distract himself he got up from the *kotatsu* and stood before the window and looked out.

If only I could get on my bike and barrel down the road in full flight…"

"Wait, what?"

Someone was standing in front of the apartment—a rare sight for Riku these days. Reminiscent of a telephone pole, he was a tall and slender man in a black down jacket and camouflage pants.

Who is he?

To get a clearer view he plastered his face to the window. The man was quietly looking up at Riku's apartment suite. When his eyes met Riku's, though, he suddenly got restless and contorted his face and hugged himself and walked around and around in circles.

Weird!

Riku considered telling his father, but he was glued to the PC. Besides, when Riku saw how wry his father's face appeared, his will to speak to him faded.

Riku turned his eyes to look outside again, but there was nobody there now.

The Mystery Man and the Tonchi

Winter vacation this year was going to begin earlier than usual and end later than usual.

To a child such as Riku, there should have been no happier news than this, yet he absolutely could not bring himself to feel pleased. There was nothing grateful, after all, to feel about a winter vacation in which he was barred, at all times, from going outside. It had only been a few days since he'd returned from Hokkaido, but Riku was already bored to death.

His father had started to go to work at the hospital again from the fourth. Apparently, according to him, people who'd lost their family to the tsunami had become very mentally unstable.

"Some are losing their sleep, some are suffering from high blood pressure, and some are even losing their eyesight because they're so stressed…"

While his father was at work, Riku was home alone. There was nothing to do. It was, in fact, better for him to be attending school. Not even the public library was open, nor was there anywhere Riku could go to have some fun.

To kill time, he fired up his father's PC and surfed to the Fukushima Kids blog site and took a look at the photographs posted there. Riku wanted to make sure he hadn't dreamt up all those days he'd spent in Hokkaido.

There he was in the photos taken by the staff. So was Masato. So was Mr. Nomura and Mrs. Nomura and even Gen-san. Everyone was laughing. But all that was in the past now.

Riku made the PC go to sleep, letting his memories disappear.

Everyone must have forgotten about me by now, surely.

No, Riku, that can't be. Of course they remember you.

And on and on the two Rikus inside himself went, wearing Riku down.

I'm, like, such a sissy.

Riku remembered the words he wrote in the questionnaire on the last night of the tour.

Question: What experience made you feel that it was worth joining the Hokkaido tour?

"Being thanked so much. In Fukushima I was always thanking people. But when I came to Hokkaido, all sorts of people were thanking me instead. Which made me happy, because it made me feel that even I could be of some help to others."

I felt so powerful over there, like I could do anything in this world, but back home I'm just back to being a helpless child.

Ahh, this really super bugs me. I want to ride my bike fast. To hell with radiation! I want to breathe all the fresh air I can and move around freely with all my strength.

Riku jumped to his feet and yelled, "I can't go on like this anymore!"

He put on his down jacket, wrapped a muffler around his neck, and wore his sneakers.

He found his bicycle abandoned in the corridor of the apartment building, unridden since he'd returned.

I'm going to let it rip.

Carrying the bike with him, Riku climbed down the stairs and went out the first-floor entrance. When he was about to straddle his bike, though, his heart thumped violently.

That man was there again.

That man in the black down jacket and camouflage pants, tall like a telephone pole.

He was looking Riku's way, stock-still. His hair was long and bunched at the back, just like a girl. His mouth was shaped like a mask that looked like a crow's beak.

His eyes, which were darting here and there restlessly above the mask, were sunken, and his complexion was like the color of a mud wall.

Since Riku had appeared suddenly, the man, too,

seemed surprised. It was midwinter, but his forehead was bubbling with beads of sweat slowly trickling down from the temples to his chin.

When Riku said, "Can I help you?" the man replied, "Uhh…" before pressing down on his chest with both his hands and crouching down painfully.

"Are you all right?" Riku cried out, still carrying his bike.

"Wh-Where are you going?" the man said, lifting his face and gazing at Riku with concern.

"Where…? What do you mean, where?"

"Don't ride that bicycle. You'll die if you do. Don't you feel sick? Don't you feel nauseous?"

"No, not really…" Riku said, taking a breath to check how he was feeling.

"Don't breathe!" The man yelled in a tearful voice. "Look at me! My body is in such a terrible state because of the radiation. I can barely even stand now. I'm warning you, if you breathe you're going to die."

Riku, alarmed, held his breath while having no idea what to do now.

"Is the doctor there?" the man asked while going into a coughing fit.

"You mean my father?" Riku said, breathing again at last.

"Oh, you must be Doctor Sato's son. Look, I want to see the doctor. I think he'll believe me. Radiation is bad for the health. Unless we all get away from here as soon as possible, everyone's going to suffer like me."

Could it be that this man's so afraid of the radiation that

he's breaking into a cold sweat?

Come to think of it, he's shivering too.

"My father has gone to the hospital. He's not here."

"He wasn't at the hospital a while ago…"

"I'm not lying. He's been gone since morning. I suppose he's making a house call somewhere, like he usually does to one of those homes in the temporary housing area."

"Look, I need to see the doctor," he said before sinking to the ground.

"Are you okay? Get a grip, mister." Riku approached him, but the man reeked like anything, like he hadn't taken a bath in a long while.

Riku called his father on the cell phone.

After several rings his father finally answered.

"Dad? There's a man here who's come to see you. What should I tell him?"

His father, raising his voice, said, "What?" He sounded very stern, as if he was scowling.

When Riku said, "He's tall and thin and has long hair," he seemed to immediately recognize who the man was.

"The man seems very ill."

"I see. What's this person doing now?"

"He's resting at the *kotatsu*."

"What? You let him into our apartment?" His father yelled so loudly that Riku spontaneously yanked the phone away from his ear.

"Well, because he seemed to be suffering so much."

The hubbub of the hospital commotion was leaking through the phone: Doctor Sato… someone's voice was saying.

"All right," his father said, sounding very nervous now. "I'll be heading home right away."

The call got cut off.

The man, having sipped some water Riku had served him, seemed to have calmed down a little. That water was sent by Aunt Midori, and it was safe, since it was from a foreign country.

Riku asked, "Would you like some hot tea?"

The man said, in a courteous manner contrary to his appearance, "No thank you. That won't be necessary. I'm sorry to have troubled you."

Then, the man suddenly became restless and stood up.

"I'm really sorry to have troubled you," he said. "I'll be taking your leave now."

Riku tried to stop him. "My father's on his way, so he won't be long now," but the man went on to quickly wear his shoes. As he was doing so, Riku saw that the tip of his socks were torn so that his big toes were saying hello.

"Thank… thank you," he said again, "for being so kind to me today."

When the man politely bowed, he felt dizzy again and leaned on the wall, before getting a grip on himself and grasping the doorknob and, apparently with a firm resolve, opening the door with full force and dashing outside.

Looking down from the window, Riku saw that the man seemed like he was really going to die; he was staggering while walking back, and coughing many times, taking a rest now and then.

He came to see Father, Riku thought, so why was he

going home now?

Riku called his father again.

"That person I told you about? Well, he's gone."

Riku's father seemed very preoccupied. "I see. All right. If anything else comes up, just give me another call. Oh, and one more thing…" he said, before adding with a little anger, "From now on, don't let him into the house again, understand?"

Fighting the urge, for a moment, to rebel against his father's words, Riku fell silent. They didn't sound like something his father would say, not the father Riku knew, who never spoke in that tone of voice.

That night, after returning from the hospital, his father seemed restless, looking out the window over and over again. Was it because of that man who was tall and thin like a telephone pole?

"That person's afraid of radiation. He's become convinced that the radiation is making him ill, so the symptoms have started to appear for real."

"So there's nothing wrong with him?"

"Humans, you see, can get sick from the mind. There's a saying that goes, Care killed the cat, right? That basically means that worry is often the cause of illness, that sickness and health start from the mind."

"So then you can't get sick from radiation exposure?"

"I can't say that you can't ever get sick that way, but… don't you worry."

"Why can't kids go outside and play then?"

Riku's father kept quiet for a while, until he finally said,

"Look, nobody understands the effects of radiation that well yet. So for the time being it's better to take precautions."

So it's dangerous, after all. And that's why everybody's moving out.

"Radiation is invisible, right? It's something you can't see with your own eyes. And what you can't see, frightens you, right? Just like ghosts. When you start believing in and worrying over things you can't see, you trouble not only yourself, but those around you too, like that man you let into the apartment today."

You can't compare radiation to a ghost, Riku thought. They're different. Besides, as Gen-san said, you have to be polite to whatever or whoever you meet.

"That man wasn't a bad person, you know."

"I know that," Riku's father said a little sadly. "He's sick and he needs treatment. But right now your father doesn't have the time to listen to his stories…"

Two, three days later, the man was standing outside again.

Riku pretended not to notice, but he became somewhat concerned, nonetheless, since the man was standing there and looking Riku's way all the time. When, by chance, Riku looked down, their eyes met. The man, with his face twitching, waved.

What a strange person! To avoid eye contact Riku turned around, and then sighed.

The man appeared unsteady and in poor health as before. What's more, today he had a bump over his right eye and seemed to be in much pain.

When his eyes met Riku's again, he waved flimsily.

Riku too, reluctantly, waved back, before thinking, Whoops, and returned to ignoring the man by playing his video game at the *kotatsu* table. Still, Riku couldn't stop himself from getting worried and looking outside again. The man was still standing there. What should I do? Riku wondered, while also feeling sort of very sorry for him.

When Riku went down and the man saw him, he began to get restless again. "You must not go outside. You're still just a child!" he said pushing Riku back into the first-floor entrance of the apartment building and shutting the door behind him. Then, after letting out a sigh of relief—going "Phew!"—he wiped the sweat off his forehead.

"My father's at the hospital today too."

The man leaned against the wall and looked at Riku painfully. "I see, I see. Thank you."

The man was, just like the other time, sweating a lot even though it was the middle of winter. In fact, he was perspiring so much that beads of sweat were dripping down to his feet, so Riku asked, "Are you okay?"

"Yeah. I'm okay. It's just that my health has been completely ruined by the radiation. I'm not from here, you see—I'm not a local. I only happened to be here for work when the earthquake hit, and that's when I got exposed to the radiation, you see. So I'm a victim. You understand that, don't you?"

The man's breath blew over Riku's face, as Riku mulled over what to say to him.

"But it's not just me. You're a victim too, right? Right?" When Riku continued to just stand there with his mouth shut, the man began to cough and, after pulling out a throat spray, he opened his mouth wide to squirt and sterilize.

"This town has been contaminated. It's imperative to have everyone evacuated as soon as possible. But no matter how many times I keep saying so, nobody listens. But we're all in grave danger. Listen to me, the mere fact that you're living here can deceive the world into thinking that radiation is safe. When that happens, Japan will be ruined."

The man, unable to keep standing any longer, crouched down to the concrete floor at last.

"Before people end up like me, everybody must leave here. This is what I want to tell your father, this is what I must warn him. Only your father was willing to listen to me, you know."

The bruise over the man's eye burst and began to bleed.

Riku said, "I'll be right back," and hightailed it back to his room before returning with a Band-Aid. When Riku fixed the bandage over his wound, the man jumped up and down dramatically and hollered, "Ow, Ow, Ow."

He's kind of a wimp, Riku thought, amused.

"When I told the residents around here that they needed to flee at once because if they didn't they were all going to die from radiation exposure, they gave me a black eye, beating me like savages, hitting and kicking me over and over again. There's a brainwashing campaign going on. It's terrifying."

The man suddenly lifted his face and, opening his eyes wide, said, "Wha-what's that on your shoulder?"

When Riku turned his head to the side, wondering

what the man was talking about, there, perched on his right shoulder, was the tonchi.

No way…!

The tonchi's huge, almond-shaped eyes of black glittered as he flashed a grin.

"Ahh!" Riku screamed in surprise as he attempted to hide the tonchi with his hands, but the tonchi ran around this way and that and, this time, jumped onto Riku's left shoulder.

"Is that a dog? No, it can't be. But it's not a monkey either…"

Riku, panicking, said, "This is my pet, a really rare breed found only in South America."

The tonchi, who was sitting on Riku's head now, was cocking his head to the side, looking puzzled, as he stared at the man.

Then, without any warning, he leaped onto the man's head and, with a bounce, hurled himself into the air before landing smack on the palm of the man's hand.

"He's, he's on my hand!" the man cried, utterly thrilled.

Riku was helpless, left with nothing more to do, but watch the tonchi—on top of the man's hand—begin to dance, wiggling his long arms and legs.

"Look, he's laughing. He's looking at me and laughing. What a friendly fellow this creature is!"

Riku saw the man laugh for the first time. He looked so happy.

Still, why was the tonchi here anyway? And how did he get here?

The man was ecstatic now, watching the tonchi and

saying, "How cute!" while squirming with joy, his cheeks suddenly blushing with a reddish tinge. While playing with the tonchi, he seemed to have gotten slightly healthier too; the tonchi, with his tiny hands, was fiddling with the man's nose, performing his masterful handstand for him, and moving around in hilarious ways.

Ha, ha, ha, the man began to laugh out loud.

He must be really happy, Riku thought. He must have been very lonely too. And that's why he sees the tonchi.

"The sight of this creature is so uplifting!" The man blew his nose into his handkerchief and began to sob. "I haven't had this much fun in a long while, not since the earthquake."

Then the tonchi, from the man's hand, suddenly dropped down to the ground. Although the man tried to catch him in a hurry, the tonchi was too nimble, bouncing here and there before finally leaping out the entrance.

The door at the entrance, even though nobody had laid a hand on it, had opened by itself like an automatic door, letting in blustery gusts of wind.

The man, standing to his feet, yelled, "No, don't! "It's contaminated outside!" and began to run in hot pursuit after the tonchi. Riku, too, joined the chase in a panic.

The man was running out of breath, gasping and panting, as the tonchi, passing through the alley, reached the main street and headed in the direction of the building of the town office. Nonetheless, the man doggedly tried to keep up with the tonchi, staggering and falling down on his knees many times.

Apparently, other people didn't see the tonchi; the

passersby, wearing dubious expressions on their face, were turning around and doing double takes on the man.

There was such a huge crowd gathered around in front of the town office that the scene looked like a festival.

A closer look, though, showed that the people there were newspaper reporters with cameras and government officials in neat business suits. Surrounding these people, in turn, were a gathering of the citizens of Minamisōma, among whom were the faces of Riku's classmates.

What's going on? Riku wondered, as he came to a standstill before the gates of the town office.

When the man came running down the sidewalk, wobbling, somebody spotted him and shouted, "It's him! That's the guy who's been spreading false rumors, telling everyone that this town has become too contaminated to live in."

All eyes fell on the man at once, the photographers pointing their camera lens at him and snapping away.

The crowd began to make accusations: "You're causing trouble for everybody!" "You're filled with nothing but lies!"

Frightened out of his mind, the man began to sweat tremendously, breaking into a coughing fit and squirting his medicinal spray into his throat as his legs shivered.

Riku started feeling very sorry for the man.

He's sick, Riku thought. Sick from so much worrying that it was messing up his mind.

Then, at that time, from the town office building, appeared the mayor, accompanied by his entourage. Even Riku could see, as everyone's eyes shifted from the man to the mayor, that he seemed like an important, urban politician.

A group holding the banner that read "No Nuclear Power!" went into a wild uproar: "Why are you standing by and doing nothing while Minamisōma dies?"

"Give us back our land, give us back our homes!" everyone cried out chanting.

Riku understood how angry the grownups were; they all had the same look Riku saw on his father's face, the same cynical look of mistrust.

Riku felt sort of sad, and wondered what he could do to help soothe their rage.

How wonderful it would be, he thought, if everyone could live happily together, just like in Hokkaido.

The tonchi wasn't there anymore. He had vanished and gone somewhere.

Approaching from behind were a large number of voices crying out, "Don't abandon Fukushima!" "Stop nuclear power generation!"

Riku found the man crouched down at the traffic light of an intersection and tugged at his hand. "Come on, let's go. It's dangerous out here. You could get run over by a car."

The man, as Riku forcibly pulled him up, mumbled in a hopeless voice, "That poor creature! He'll get killed by the radiation."

Annoyed, Riku yelled, "He's fine! He's not going to die. I'm one hundred percent sure about that."

"How can you be so damn sure? You're all fools! Can't

you see you're being tricked?" The man shook off Riku's hand and walked away, like a sleepwalker, in the opposite direction to the town office, while declaring, "This is the end of the world…"

Ahh, go ahead and stay sick. See if I care!

Riku was about to stomp off in anger, when, once again, the tonchi appeared out of nowhere and followed the man, hoppity-hopping towards him and, after approaching his feet, springing up and alighting on the man's shoulder. Then, flashing a grin, the tonchi waved back at Riku, as the man, still unawares of the tonchi, went on mumbling and grumbling as ever.

But when the tonchi tugged at the man's ear a few times, he finally noticed and hollered "Ahh" in surprise, before his knees gave way and he sank to the ground.

The tonchi continued riding on the man's head, as he wiggled his body and pressed his face against the man's forehead.

"Aww, so cute!" The man delightfully placed the tonchi on the palm of his hand and began rubbing cheeks with the little guy.

Are you a kid or what? Riku wondered. Still, taking in the situation, he felt tender and compassionate again and was able to return to the center of his being; the place inside himself where he felt calm and cheerful, just as he did when he'd climbed the snowy mountain with Mr. Nomura.

This is who I really am, Riku realized.

I Will Be Here

The long winter vacation was over, and school had finally started again.

The school bus was the same old same old. The group commute was the same old same old. The mask was the same old same old. But Riku still looked forward to meeting his classmates for the first time in a long time.

When Riku entered the classroom—brightly saying "Good morning!"—a group of boys were talking in whispers while looking Riku's way, their eyes immediately betraying to Riku that they were all ridiculing him. It was somewhat unpleasant.

One boy then approached Riku and said, "Hey, Sato! You and that guy friends or something?"

"What guy?"

Looking uneasy, the boy answered, "I'm talking about that slightly crazy guy, the one who's been spreading nothing but lies…"

Oh, Riku realized. Come to think of it, this boy was in front of the town office that time, too.

"Look, he's not a friend. He's just been to my apartment once."

All the boys exchanged glances with each other and smirked.

"Well, I figured you must be friends with that nut job since you're not originally a Fukushima native."

Riku felt like he'd been stabbed—So this is what I've been to them all this time: an outsider.

"You really didn't want to come here anyway, right?"

"Yeah, so don't you think it's about time for you as well to just get the hell out of here and scuttle back home to Utsunomiya?"

Mr. Iwamoto entered the classroom.

Everybody returned to their seat, though all eyes were still on Riku, glaring with suspicion.

After surveying the classroom, Mr. Iwamoto fixed his eyes on Riku's face, but Riku turned away. Even after homeroom session began, Riku was unable to concentrate at all, his temples throbbing with a tingling sensation, his body becoming hard as stone.

"With the start of the new year," Mr. Iwamoto began, "the town has finally started to take steps in earnest towards a full-scale revival. Your teachers and parents are working hard together to swiftly restore the school to its former glory. I'm sure this will be challenging for all of you too, but let's all join forces and bring back the original Minamisōma Elementary School."

The original Minamisōma Elementary School…?

What kind of place was that?

Riku, who had moved into this area only after the disaster struck, had no idea.

To Riku, Minamisōma was, from the beginning, a town without people. Here, everyone wore masks, long-sleeved shirts, and full-length pants, never shorts. Here, nobody ate any food produced locally. Here, water was bought and drunk. Here, you couldn't play in the playground. This was the Minamisōma Riku knew.

Even so, Riku didn't think about leaving the town. Even if the lunch was lousy, the radiation levels high, to Riku, such problems didn't matter that much.

The people of Minamisōma were kind to Riku, and that's why Riku liked being here. But, now, perhaps, things had changed…"

Once again a poisonous, black stain spread throughout Riku's heart.

During lunch break, Riku was sitting on the bench by the gymnasium's storage shed, when Mr. Iwamoto came over.

"We're in January now, so it's really cold, isn't it?"

Riku was resting his head on his knees, his face completely concealed by a muffler and a hat and a mask.

Even if it was cold, or even if the radiation level was high, it was better to be out here than inside the classroom.

"I like the cold, because I like snow."

"Is that right?" Mr. Iwamoto said and sat next to Riku.

He must be worried about me, Riku thought.

The teacher blew breath into his hands and rubbed them together. His burdock-like hands, Riku thought, were the hands of someone who's been working all the time. In fact, they were just like Mr. Nomura's and Gen-san's hands. Mr. Iwamoto's like a huge mountain. When I'm together with him, I feel relaxed.

"Everyone's been coping for so long now, so it's no wonder that the fatigue is starting to show." The teacher seemed to be talking to himself.

"Those guys, the boys who were picking on you, are all living in temporary residences now, unable to return to their homes. Their families, too, have been broken up, so they're frustrated. They're all good guys at heart, though."

Mr. Iwamoto, too, must be tired, Riku thought.

"So Sato, I heard you went to Hokkaido. Was it fun?"

"Yes it was."

"Great! So, what was fun about your adventure there?

"I was taught about all kinds of things about animals; about rabbits and bears. I went up the mountain and even saw a wild marten. It was golden and so beautiful!"

"Good for you!"

"I never even imagined that a rabbit couldn't cry out. I was told that, because rabbits are herbivores that get hunted and killed by other animals for food, they don't vocalize. I was also told that the living things of this world offer their lives to each other. But still, if you get eaten, you'll suffer, I think; I mean, you'll feel pain, right?"

Mr. Iwamoto was listening to Riku's story in silence.

"Mr. Iwamoto, you used to raise cows, right? Even cows are raised to be eaten by humans, right? Why do living things have to offer their lives to each other? Is God mean?"

"Ha, ha, ha. Is God mean, eh?"

"I mean, like, after all, you're born and given this precious thing called life, you know... but for what?"

"Well…"

Returning home from Hokkaido, Riku was grappling with nothing but heavy ideas like that; before he knew it, his mind would be reeling with questions for which, no matter how hard he tried, he couldn't come up with the answers.

"Why are we being let to live at all? Even I don't know the answer to that," Mr. Iwamoto mumbled as if to himself, looking up at the sky.

On March 4—a Sunday—when it was almost a year after the earthquake disaster, Riku and his father went out for a drive along the coast.

It was Riku who had asked his father to take him there. "I want to see the seashore," he had said. "Many people died there, right?"

"Why this interest all of a sudden?" his father asked, surprised.

"I don't know, but I want to see what it's like out there. I hate it that I don't really know anything about what took place in Minamisōma. I just want to know, even if only a little."

Screwing up his eyes, Riku's father peered into Riku's face and said, "Understood."

It was a very powerful "understood," happily reassuring Riku that something had reached his father, that something had struck a chord in him.

"The seashores of Minamisōma were devastated by the tsunami; houses and fields, and a large number of people were all swallowed up by the waves. The fire brigade were going to their rescue, but the nuclear accident happened and the government issued an evacuation order. So they couldn't reach those who may have still been alive at the time. To this day, the citizens of this place are filled with regret. They have survivor's guilt, feeling sorry that they were the only ones to have survived."

The school bus driver had told Riku, with his eyelids creased, "Don't you ever go to the seaside, you hear?"

By car, from the house to the coast, the trip didn't take even ten minutes. Midway through, the road began to meander and get bumpy, making the car spring up and down, going boing, boing. After moving ahead for a time, a gigantic wall of garbage came into view.

"That's the debris," Riku's father explained. "They're gathering all the debris and piling it up like that."

Mountain after mountain of debris lined the shoreline, where the power shovels were busy piling up the loads being transported by trucks. These mountains were so huge, in fact, that the mechanical shovels appeared like toys.

"What's going to happen to all this debris?"

"Who knows? Even the debris—all that rubble—has been exposed to radiation."

The two of them stand on an embankment that had collapsed after the earthquake caused it to crack. Apparently, the place was once a bustling beach resort.

"For the time being, there won't be anybody stepping into the sea."

"For the time being? How long's that?"

"Nobody knows yet."

Abandoned on the vast expanse of a field, which looked as if its surface had been scraped off, were fishing boats that had been washed ashore; vehicles that had been submerged; houses stripped down to their skeletal framework, and houses that had been flattened, their furniture and household effects completely washed away and probably buried by now in one of the mountains of debris.

"Look," Riku's father said. "The grass has already grown so tall. This is life in all its powerful glory, so resilient and strong! Come summer, the blades will be even thicker."

Stepping out of the car, Riku desperately tried, while watching the trucks coming and going from the mountains of debris, to sense what had taken place here. But, beyond the scenery he beheld, he couldn't understand anything.

An incredibly terrible thing has happened, Riku thought. Many people have died. Yet I go on living as if nothing has happened.

The sea was a deep shade of blue, so very big and so very quiet.

In April, Riku would be in the sixth grade.

Today, Riku realized, he was nearly as tall as his father.

With the beginning of the new school term came, once again, a flood of volunteers to the school.

There were many who were visiting from distant lands, including America, France, Germany, Italy, Bangladesh, Brazil, Hong Kong, China, Korea—such a great variety of humanity that you couldn't be blamed for believing that the whole wide world was heading for the little old town of Minamisōma.

Among the international volunteers, the trio from Italy were hugely popular with the children. They visited many times, baking pizzas for the kids, sharing chocolates and candies that were as colorful as jewels, and even singing songs for them. Always bright and bubbly, they would do all they could to cheer them up.

One of them—a photographer who looked like Santa Claus with his great big paunch and dazzling white mustache—spoke Japanese fantastically well.

He would trudge around the school, saying, Ciao! and make the children laugh with his jokes while capturing them in action on his video camera. Apparently, he was going to broadcast the video to a worldwide audience.

The camera was pointed at Riku too.

"Hi there! How's life? Have you been happy these days?"

Riku paused to think.

"No," he finally answered, "I haven't been that happy."

"Oh my! Now why is that? What's bothering you the most?"

"That I can't play outside... and..."

"And?"

"That everybody's quarrelling with each other."

An image of Riku's gloomy face was showing in close-up in Santa Claus's viewfinder, as he lowered his camera and smiled.

"You're a kind boy, aren't you?"

Riku felt that this person saw a child as an equal to him. He even smelled the same as Mr. Nomura and Gen-san.

"I don't know anything, but I still want to know what's real."

"You mean the truth?"

"Yes. Children have the right to know the truth too, I think."

"You know what? That's a fair opinion. In Rome, an eleven-year old is already considered an adult."

Then, pulling out a laptop from his bag, Santa Claus lifted the lid open and positioned the screen before Riku.

"Pay attention, okay? What I'm about to show you is top-secret footage I shot."

All of a sudden, movie trailer-like music begins to play—Da-dum!—followed by a fast-talking voiceover, probably Italian. Although Riku doesn't understand a word of what the narrator is saying, he's transfixed by the screen, which fluoresces with images of spectacles and scenes he's already seen on TV many times: the exploding building of the Fukushima Daiichi Nuclear Power Station; roads greatly congested with evacuating cars; the soldiers of the Self-Defense Forces with gasmasks attached; the nuclear reactor building being hosed down with water; a man making a complicated analysis, saying, "Radioactive contamination has spread over a wide range of…"; a close-up of the Prime Minister's face; the press conference scene showing the people of Tokyo Electric Power all lined up and taking a bow; a mother, holding her baby in her arms, saying, "What's going to happen to us?"; an emergency shelter partitioned off with cardboard boxes; school—Riku's school; children wearing masks; the blue plastic bags in the playground; men in white hazmat suits measuring radiation levels around the campus, holding up the dosimeter to the camera and remarking how high the reading is; children exercising in the gymnasium; even the lousy lunch appears on the screen.

…Wait, a field of grass. The camera pans into a white hut there; pitch black darkness; a flashlight flashes on.

Huh? What are those brown objects?

Riku, without intending to, leans forward.

Cows. Hundreds of cows, all dried up like mummies.

The camera now captures the scene outside the hut; a large number of cows are dead, collapsed on the road and inside thickets of grass. Corpses of cats, dogs, and pigs also come into view.

Perhaps Mr. Iwamoto's Baytaro was there too.

The dosimeter is constantly beeping; a grandmother in the emergency shelter cries, "I want to go home"; destroyed homes; mountains of debris lining a shoreline—Hey, I was there the other day.

Many people are crying before rows of white boxes.

Hey, I know what they are. They're the boxes to put dead people inside.

When Mother died they put her in a box just like that

before setting it on fire.

The shore is lined up with so many boxes there's hardly any room for walking.

Are these boxes empty? Or are they…

"The TV never showed anything like that!"

Santa Claus said, "That's because the Japanese TV media are weak-kneed" and shut the lid of the laptop.

"Tell me, is radiation really dangerous?"

"Levels around the coast and in forests are high. But inside the town, it's nothing serious. In this town you get very powerful gusts of wind, so radioactive materials get blown off and start to drift in the air, you see, and after getting mixed with the rain and snow, they fall here and there in other areas. Why, you can find places with even higher radiation levels than here. It's not a matter of distance really."

Then, Santa Claus, lifting his forefinger, said, "But just because the level is low here, it doesn't mean that everything is okay."

Riku nodded.

"Seen from overseas, the entire nation of Japan is in danger. But then again, during the Cold War era, the United States and the Soviet Union were repeatedly conducting nuclear tests. So seen from outer space, the entire Earth is in danger." Santa Claus, with outstretched hands, laughed, ho, ho, ho.

This person hasn't lost hope. Why?

Why were there, in this world, two kinds of people: the hopeful, bright kind and the despairing, gloomy kind who worried all the time? They both live in the same world, so what makes them so worlds apart?

"I moved into this place two months after the accident," Riku said.

"Is that right…? Now why did you do that?"

"Because of my father's work. He's a doctor, you see."

Hugging Riku's head with his big, hairy arms, Santa Claus said, "On top of being kind, you're brave. There's a saying, you know, that goes like this: Unless you're strong, you can't stay alive. Unless you're kind, there's no value in staying alive."

And then he winked.

"So long, boy. Let's meet again somewhere in the world. Ciao!"

On the head of Santa's receding form, Riku saw… a bird? Huh? No. Tonchi!

Riku rubbed his eyes, but the mountain god was still there, blinking his eyes of black and flashing a grin at Riku and forming a V sign with his tiny fingers.

Santa Claus was humming, though, apparently unaware of the tonchi.

The tonchi was invisible to him…

Surely, Riku thought, the tonchi intends to travel around the world with Santa Claus.

Riku quietly waved at the tonchi and, suddenly realizing the gravity of the moment, stood at attention, back erect, and saluted.

Goodbye Tonchi, and thank you.

Aunt Midori was angry, because Riku never visited her in Yokohama during the winter vacation, not even once.

Riku believed that, no matter how bored he got, it was better to stay at home than go to Yokohama, where he'd be stripped naked and washed like a dirty animal...

"Sure, you were away in Hokkaido, but it was just for a week, wasn't it? You should have come to Yokohama during the holidays."

As ever, Aunt Midori's telephone call was long.

Riku understood that she was worried about him. For that, he was grateful. But at the same time, he was also very annoyed by all of her worrying, clearly realizing now, without fail, how he truly hated phone calls from her.

"I understand that the radiation levels over there are still high. So why don't you transfer to a school in Yokohama this April? Remember, from next year you already need to start preparing for your junior high school entrance exams, so it's best that you enroll into a prep school. Here in Yokohama, there are plenty of good ones you can choose from."

Junior high exams...oh yeah, that's right, I'll be in junior high next year. Wow! Unbelievable. I can't wrap my head around that at all.

"If you think about what's good for your future, you should absolutely come to Yokohama. I'm sure that's what my big sister would tell you to do, if she were still alive today."

Aunt Midori was positive, but Riku wondered, if Mother were still alive, what would she really tell me? Surely, she'd say, 'Do as you please, Riku.' Yes, that's what I feel she would tell me.

Because, 'It's your life, Riku. Nobody can live it for you,

except you. So live it with all your strength, with all your heart, knowing how precious you really are.' That's what Mother always used to say; it was her pet phrase.

Perhaps those words were meant for herself too, to remind herself of their wisdom, having been born physically frail.

"Aunt Midori, I'm going to stay here in Minamisōma. I'm not going to Yokohama."

"Why not? Is it because you get so lonely when you're not with your father? Is that it?"

"No, it's not that. It's just that I like being here; it's even fun being here. Sure, life in this town can get tough, but I also think it's an amazing experience! That's why I'm not going to Yokohama."

Aunt Midori lost her head and went ballistic, squealing hysterically: "Why, you insolent little brat, sounding like you know what you're talking about; oh for goodness sake, ooh, ooh, ooh!" she fumed, bellowing like a cow.

"What are you going to do if you get sick?"

"Well, my mother was sick, right? She was born physically weak, right? Is that, like, a bad thing?"

"That's not the issue here."

"Guess what? You're going to die someday, too, Aunt Midori. Why do you keep saying things that only frighten us? We're living here, you know. In Hokkaido, everybody was kind, and because of that, I became very well. I want to be somebody positive, somebody who can encourage other people. I want to do work that will cheer people up and energize everybody. If I go there to Yokohama, I'm afraid I might turn into someone else, someone I'm really not. I'm staying here, Auntie. I'm happy Dad and I moved here."

"Fine! Do as you please!!" She hung up, slamming the phone down.

Riku's father, who had been staring at the PC, slowly raised his head and laughed.

"Now, that's what I call a breakdown in negotiations."

"Yup."

Riku returned the cell phone to his father.

"You win, Riku!"

"What?"

"You're absolutely right. In fact, you've opened my eyes too. Some lessons can only be learned here and nowhere else. I say, it must have been our destiny to come here. You made me remember that. Thank you, Riku."

Ah, come on, Dad! You're embarrassing me.

With both his hands, Riku's father received the punch Riku threw at him—I'm gonna getcha! I'm gonna getcha!

"Not bad, hey, watch it!"

The two of them sang together loudly for the first time in a long time. Good, good, good, good vibrations!

"Whoops! I just remembered, new residents have just moved in," Riku's father said in a panic, his hand clamped over his mouth.

That evening Riku finally got around to writing back to Natsumi Suzuki in Utsunomiya. Indeed, his reply had ended up being eight months in the making.

To Miss Natsumi Suzuki:

I'm sorry for replying so late to your letter. I'm doing well in Minamisōma. Many shops are still closed, and we still can't play at school in the playground, but all kinds of things are getting better little by little. Though some say it's getting worse, I think things are improving. Right now, only a few people live in the town. The ones who have left, and the ones staying behind all have different opinions of their own, so I can't clearly tell what's real and what's not. But many people from all over the world come here. I even met folks from Africa and from Arabia, too! Everyone's friendly.

Oh, by the way, how's Jones the rabbit? You know, when Jones kicks the ground with his hind legs? Well, it seems that he's sensing danger, not dancing.

I've never put myself in Jones's shoes. I've never thought about his feelings. But now, I want to become the kind of person who understands how animals feel, the kind of person who sees what goes on in their mind.

But not only animals. I want to understand how humans think and feel too.

I suppose moving to this town has got me wondering about such things. It's a very strange and wonderful place.

Please come and see me sometime, Natsumi. It'll be fun.

Riku Sato
11 March, 2012

Afterword

On Writing "Riku and the Kingdom of White"

My involvement with the project, "Fukushima Kids," began when I had the good fortune of getting to know Mr. Hirohiko Yoshida, who, at that time, was promoting this project that aimed to help bring the children of Fukushima to long-term, open-air schools, where they could come into contact with nature. Specifically, I had the privilege of helping out with the project's PR and fund-raising campaigns.

Thanks to the fact that Mr. Yoshida is blessed with an extensive network, which he had built over his many years of working as a professional engaged in children's social education and hands-on learning, the project team was able to put together a very well-rounded program that made it possible for children to spend their days freely amid invigorating, natural surroundings.

Run by a total of 4,600 volunteers, the enterprise was slated to last, from its inception, for five years.

By April, 2011, the project had gotten off to a swift

start, and by the summer of that year, it saw 518 students studying in the great outdoors, and in the course of those five years, that number had jumped to more than 4,800. In those early days, I couldn't even begin to imagine what shape this enterprise would take five years hence.

Finally, though, this year saw the Fukushima Kids project usher in its fifth year, bringing it to a close.

On the occasion of its completion, however, I received a challenge from the administrators: "We want you to write a novel about the children of Fukushima."

They had decided that the best way to convey what the children felt about the time they spent in the learning program, and the lessons they had learned through their immersive experiences in nature, was not through a report, but through the narrative arc of a story.

And so, having been involved in the project since it was launched, I was privileged with the task of collecting data and interviewing the children who participated in the "Fukushima Kids" program and, thereafter, writing this novel. In the course of my research, I met many children and their parents, all of whom were local residents who had stayed behind in Fukushima since the accident.

While the matter of radiation levels continued to be a large concern, everyone was, at the same time, burdened with a host of other harrowing problems, including job loss and the loss of their homes, family members and relatives. Nonetheless, the people I met were all cheerful and upbeat. I was also struck by how the children delightfully told me that they were happy to have remained in Fukushima.

Furthermore, people living in Fukushima, and those

looking at Fukushima from the outside, diverged greatly, I felt, with respect to the level of concern. Since I am an outsider, I naturally cannot relate, on a personal level, to the challenges and difficulties the people of Fukushima face every day.

Nonetheless, my heart was swayed by the solidarity—the caring concern—shared among those who had resolved to live and bring up their children in Fukushima; by the lengths they went to protect their children; and by the courage they showed in the face of confronting their challenges.

The importance of coming into touch with people through experiencing community in a natural environment will be demonstrated all the more in the future by each and every child who has gained this precious experience.

To the staff of "Fukushima Kids", and to the many fathers and mothers and their children who gave me their precious cooperation by consenting to be interviewed, I would like to extend my sincerest, heartfelt gratitude.

And thank you to everyone around Japan and the world, who, through the project, offered their warm encouragement to the children.

My heartfelt thanks also goes to Ms. Eriko Furukawa of KINOBOOKS for willingly consenting to the serialization of this novel and for cheering me on during the writing.

RANDY TAGUCHI
11 September, 2015